BOARDING SCHOOL MYSTERIES

FADING TRACKS

Other books in the growing Faithgirlz!™ Library

Boarding School Mysteries
Secrets for Sale (Book Two)
Smoke Screen (Book Three)
Pick Your Poison (Book Four)

The Sophie series
Sophie's World (Book One)
Sophie's Secret (Book Two)
Sophie and the Scoundrels (Book Three)
Sophie's Irish Showdown (Book Four)
Sophie's First Dance? (Book Five)
Sophie's Stormy Summer (Book Six)
Sophie Breaks the Code (Book Seven)
Sophie Tracks a Thief (Book Eight)
Sophie Flakes Out (Book Nine)
Sophie Loves Jimmy (Book Ten)
Sophie Loses the Lead (Book Eleven)
Sophie's Encore (Book Twelve)

The Blog On series
Grace Notes (Book One)
Love, Annie (Book Two)
Just Jazz (Book Three)
Storm Rising (Book Four)
Grace Under Pressure (Book Five)
Upsetting Annie (Book Six)
Jazz Off-Key (Book Seven)
Storm Warning (Book Eight)

Other books by Kristi Holl

What's A Girl to Do?
Shine on, Girl! Devotions to Keep You Sparkling
Girlz Rock: Devotions for You
Chick Chat: More Devotions for Girls
No Boys Allowed: Devotions for Girls

Check out www.faithgirlz.com

faiThGirLz!™
2 corinthians 4:18

BOARDING SCHOOL MYSTERIES
FADING TRACKS

KRISTI HOLL

ZONDERkidz

ZONDERVAN.com/
AUTHORTRACKER
follow your favorite authors

Fading Tracks
Copyright © 2008 by Kristi Holl
Illustrations © 2008 by Bruce Emmett

Requests for information should be addressed to:
Zonderkidz, *Grand Rapids, Michigan* 49530

Library of Congress Cataloging-in-Publication Data

Holl, Kristi.
     Fading Tracks / by Kristi Holl.
        p. cm. -- (Faithgirlz) (Boarding school mysteries ; bk. 1)
     Summary: When the Landmark School for Girls' van carrying an art
teacher and six students disappears near an ice-covered lake on the
way back from a field trip, twelve-year-old Jeri desperately wants to
help but everything she tries seems to make the situation worse.
     ISBN 978-0-310-71429-3 (softcover)
     [1. Missing persons--Fiction. 2. Kidnapping--Fiction. 3. Reporters
and reporting--Fiction. 4. Schools--Fiction. 5. Christian life--Fiction. 6.
Virginia--Fiction.] I. Title.
    PZ7.H7079Fad 2008
    {Fic}--dc22   2007030103

Editor: Barbara Scott
Art direction & cover design: Sarah Molegraaf
Interior design: Carlos Eluterio Estrada

Printed in the United States of America

08 09 10 11 12 • 5 4 3 2 1

So we fix our eyes not on what is seen, but what is unseen.
For what is seen is temporary, but what is unseen is eternal.

— 2 Corinthians 4:18

TABLE OF CONTENTS

1

LANDMARK SCHOOL FOR GIRLS

Thursday, 5:22 p.m. to 6:16 p.m.

Twelve-year-old Jeri McKane tore the Landmark School calendar off the wall. The rows of giant red Xs blurred as the calendar sailed through the air. Each X in February had marked a day closer to Parents' Weekend at the end of the month. Only now it wouldn't happen—at least, not for *her*.

Jeri read the message on her computer screen again.

> Hi, Sweetie. It breaks my heart, but I can't
> make it for Parents' Weekend. It's a two-day
> drive to Virginia, then two days for the activi-
> ties, plus another two-day drive back to Iowa.

Carol, my boss, said I can't be gone that long—not
while sales are down so much—and I can't afford
to fly. I'm so disappointed. I'll call soon, and I'll
be praying for us both. Love and hugs, Mom

Jeri slumped in her chair, biting her lip. When this
kind of thing happened, she felt so lonely and homesick
that she was tempted to give up her precious scholarship
and move back home. She wondered again whether going
to a great school was worth traveling so far from home.
Tossing back shoulder-length hair, she dialed her mom's
cell phone.

"Mom? I got your email and—"

"—can't take your call right now, but please leave—"

"Voice mail!" Jeri disconnected.

Back at the computer, Jeri hit "reply." Her email
name, JerichoGirl, popped up, and she typed a reply:

I called but got your voice mail. Please
call me tonight. I love you, Mom.

She clicked "send." Within seconds, a new email popped
up on her screen.

This is an out-of-office auto responder. I'm

not available, but in case of emergency, con-

tact Carol at the number below.

Jeri deleted the message, trying not to let a machine make her feel rejected. If only she could talk to her roommate. Rosa's missionary parents were in Chile, and Rosa understood the longing ache that hit Jeri so hard sometimes. Where was she anyway? It was already 5:30 and nearly dark. She should have returned from her field trip over an hour ago.

The stink of wet wool socks rose from the hissing radiator under their second-floor window. Tiny clumps of snow on the socks had melted onto the wooden floor. Jeri breathed on the frosty glass and rubbed a spot clear. Leaning against the radiator, she let the heat burn through her jeans as she stared outside. A row of mini icicles hung from the eaves like frozen fringe on a shawl. In the bare dogwood below, someone had stuck a mitten on the end of a twig. In the wind, the skeletal arm beckoned at girls who hurried by.

Jeri jerked the heavy window open and grabbed her binoculars from the windowsill. The gloomy, overcast sky seemed to seep into their room. Girls dressed in blue school uniforms rushed past Hampton House on shoveled sidewalks. Leaning out, Jeri focused the binoculars and searched in both directions for her roommate's fuchsia scarf and hat.

No Rosa.

Below, a dark shape low to the ground glided toward some thick bushes. Leaning out farther, Jeri focused the binoculars there, but the animal had already disappeared behind the shrubs.

A door slammed in the hallway, making Jeri jump. She dropped the binoculars into a snow pile below.

"Good grief." Fuming, Jeri slammed the window, turning the row of tiny icicles into a shower of miniature daggers.

She raced downstairs, grabbing the newel post at the bottom to keep from falling on the polished floor. In the dorm's living room to the left, four girls studied by the crackling fire. Handmade mountain crafts decorated the heavy oak mantelpiece. Jeri grabbed her coat from one of the antique hall trees.

Outside, she retrieved her binoculars from the snowbank under her bedroom window. Light from the living room shone out, revealing the outlines of two snow angels. Four days ago, after several inches of fresh snow, Jeri had shown Rosa how to make snow angels. She smiled, thinking of Rosa flopping around in the powdery drifts.

Jeri crept toward the thick bushes, hoping the cat or dog was still there. She squatted down, and light from a street lamp revealed a couple very large paw prints. This was some fat cat, Jeri thought, poking the bushes.

"Kitty?" she said softly. "Here, kitty."

The bushes rustled, either from the freezing wind or the animal. Jeri poked a stick into the shrub. "Come out, kitty." She parted the bushes and peered through. Rats. Gone.

Shivering, she ran back inside the sixth-grade dorm and closed the heavy front door.

"Might as well leave your coat on," the house mother said, changing out of her Air Max Nikes. An athletic woman in her forties, Ms. Carter rarely missed her late afternoon workout at their fitness center. "It's time to eat."

For breakfast and supper, the sixteen girls in Hampton House walked to the dining hall with Ms. Carter and her assistant, Miss Barbara.

"Be right back." Jeri ran upstairs, left the binoculars on her bed, and then stopped at Abby and Nikki's room down the hall. Abby sat sketching at her desk, a pink goose-neck lamp spilling a pool of light on her paper.

"Chow time!" Jeri said.

Taped above Abby's desk were her drawings of castles and cathedrals, plus several photos of Abby with her mom back in Bath, England. *What a funny name for a town*, Jeri thought, *and what a long way from Landmark Hills, Virginia.*

"Coming." Abby took her blazer from the back of her chair and slipped it on. "Where's Rosa?"

"She's MIA. Her field trip was done at four, but I haven't seen her. She'd better show, 'cause she *promised* to have her advice column done on time."

For their media project, she and Rosa (along with Abby and her roommate, Nikki) were publishing a small sixth-grade newspaper. Jeri covered current events, Abby was artist and photographer, Nikki handled sports, and Rosa did the advice column. Rosa still had to write her section, and then Jeri had to format the paper and run off twenty copies ... by tomorrow morning at eight o'clock.

There was clomping on the stairs, and Nikki appeared in the doorway dressed in a black hat and leather vest. She strode to her side of the room, where walls held snapshots of her horse, Show Stopper, and a row of blue ribbons from her dressage competitions. No family photos at all, though, as if she'd been hatched from an egg.

Abby sniffed the air, her face a picture of sheer agony. "You've been in the barn. I smell horse poo on your boots!"

"You're imagining things." Nikki leaned over to check—and admire—her tooled-leather cowboy boots. Then she took off her Stetson and shook out her mane of hair. She reached for her MP3 player just as the brass bell clanged.

"Girls!" the house mother called. "Let's go!"

They hurried downstairs to line up. Miss Barbara, the twenty-five-year-old assistant, hurried them along. Her yellow and orange print shirt practically glowed in contrast to her bleached white hair. As they headed outside, Jeri thought the wind just might rip off one of Miss Barbara's fake eyelashes. Braced against the cold, Jeri fell into step behind Nikki and Abby. As they passed the bell tower, chimes played the familiar "Now the Day Is Over." Only six o'clock, and it was nearly dark already.

Suddenly a piercing snarl—almost a scream—ripped through the frigid evening air. Half a dozen girls shrieked.

Abby grabbed Jeri's arm in a viselike grip. "What was that?"

Jeri shuddered. "I don't know, but it creeps me out."

"Don't worry!" Like a mother hen, Ms. Carter gathered as many of the girls around her as she could reach. "It's just an animal out in the woods."

"That bobcat?" Nikki asked, glancing up at the wooded hills behind the school.

"Well ..." Ms. Carter hesitated. "From the sounds of it, yes. But it's a long way away."

Jeri recalled the big paw prints near the bushes and waved her hand high. "I think I saw some bobcat tracks near the dorm." Several more girls squealed. "Honest! I saw an animal outside my window just before supper. The paw prints looked like a really big cat."

"Let's keep moving." Ms. Carter shooed the girls along. "I'm sure there's nothing to worry about."

"Don't they eat meat, though?" Nikki asked.

"Yes." The house mother grimaced. "But they eat small animals—cottontails, mice, squirrels, even skunks—not girls."

Nikki lowered her voice. "They eat big animals like deer too. They sneak up on them when they're asleep." The stiff wind blew hair in her eyes. "Bobcats kill their prey by biting the animal's neck."

"That will do, Nikki," Ms. Carter called over her shoulder. "If we leave the bobcat alone, it'll leave us alone."

Jeri pulled her coat collar up and scanned both sides of the walk as they crossed the campus to the dining hall. The Virginia hills didn't have a lot of bobcats, but they'd been sighted occasionally. If Rosa were there, she'd be freaking out. "I bet Rosa's already at supper," she said to Abby. "She might be late with homework, but she's *never* late for food."

Actually, no one dared to be late to the dining hall—not if they wanted to eat. Headmistress Long—privately nick-named The Head or Head Long—had strict rules about dining hours, dress code for meals, posture while eating, and volume of conversation. Rules were made to be obeyed. Not bent. And certainly not broken.

They climbed the eight steps up to the dining hall and passed between two pillars that stood guard on either side of the front door. A massive crystal chandelier hanging from the high cathedral ceiling illuminated the entryway.

After leaving their boots and coats in the cloak room, they headed directly to their assigned tables.

Jeri scanned the room, but no Rosa. Where *was* she? For the first time, Jeri was uneasy. The van had been due back nearly two hours ago. Something must be wrong.

After getting their food, Abby and Jeri said grace silently. Jeri picked at her spinach salad. Across from her, Nikki had alfalfa sprouts stuck in her braces, as if she'd been grazing in some field.

Abby elbowed her roommate. "You've got junk hanging out your mouth."

"Sssssssssso?" Nikki asked. "Is that a p-p-problem?"

"Stop it. You know you shouldn't make fun of Houston," Abby said.

Jeri agreed. Nikki and some of the other girls often mimicked the school's stable hand, Houston Wiley, who stuttered. Houston *was* scruffy, Jeri admitted, with his thin beard and too-long jeans. But she liked him. He worked hard taking care of the horses—at least, the school's horses. Girls like Nikki, who brought her horse to school, took care of their own.

Nikki waved her fork at her roommate. "Are you g-g-gonna p-p-preach at me?"

Jeri dropped her fork with a clatter. "Since you practically live in the horse barn, I'd think you'd be nicer to Houston. Remember, the fundraiser was his idea. *You'll* probably use that fancy new Equestrian Complex more than anybody."

To raise money the last six weeks, the Landmark School girls had done many things. They'd sold candy, magazines, and nuts throughout the town. Businesses in town had donated TVs and sports equipment—even a snowmobile—that were raffled off at a basketball game. Nikki's fancy dressage riding group had performed to a sold-out audience. Each Friday, the money raised that week was announced. Several wealthy parents and some businesses had pledged to match whatever money the girls raised. The fundraising would end the next day, with matching funds due Saturday.

"You can be so mean to Houston," Jeri said.

"Like when?" Nikki protested, all wide-eyed innocence.

"Like when you locked him in the tack room, for one thing."

Nikki snorted. "Come on, it was hilarious! He was all panicky, kicking the door and yelling. A grown man!" She snickered. "I thought he'd strangle me when he finally got out."

"I would if I were him."

As she ate, Jeri glanced at the door every few minutes, but no one else arrived. She picked at her chicken and rice, and her unrest about Rosa increased. A sense of urgency nibbled now at the edges of her mind. Where was she? Why was she so late?

Abby tucked her blonde hair behind her ears. "Too bad we won't know which dorm won the candy-selling contest till tomorrow night. We could have written about that for our newspaper."

"I'm sick of the whole fundraiser," Jeri admitted, turning away from the door. "If I see Heather's dad's picture in the paper again, I'll barf."

Heather Langley's dad was one of the wealthy parents matching what the girls raised. His picture was in the Landmark School's newspaper, the *Lightning Bolt*, every Friday as he handed that week's matching check to The Head. All the other parents and businesses were giving their matching funds at the end. There'd probably just be one group photo of them.

Jeri sighed. "If only there was something *big* to investigate and report on."

"Here she goes again." Nikki scooped a mountainous glob of sour cream onto her baked potato. "Ever since that reporter talked to our class, you've been a real snoop."

Last fall a local reporter, Jake Philips, had described to their current events class how he single-handedly got several criminals arrested. "Investigative reporters *have* to snoop, or they'd never uncover anything," Jeri said.

Halfway through their peach cobbler, Headmistress Long rose and clinked her fork against her water glass until the dining hall was silent. Her face was pale, but her voice was strong. "Girls, I have an announcement. Remember, there's no cause for alarm."

Holding her breath, Jeri studied the headmistress. Her eyes were sharp and unwavering. They took in everything in the room, but gave nothing away.

"Do stay calm, ladies. There will be no hysterics."

Jeri almost choked on her cobbler. What was going on?

"She's freaking me out," Abby whispered.

Jeri nodded.

The headmistress patted her long coiled hair where it was pinned up in back. "Our school van, driven by our art teacher, Mr. Reeves, was carrying six girls home from the Fieldstone Art Museum this afternoon …" She paused to clear her throat. "There's no easy way to tell you. They've all disappeared."

2

MISSING!

Thursday, 6:17 p.m. to 10:05 p.m.

A stunned silence followed the headmistress's announcement. No cause for alarm? Was she crazy? Jeri couldn't draw a deep breath, as if all the air had been sucked out of her lungs. Thoughts raced through her mind, tumbling over each other.

Rosa wasn't late. She was *missing*.

Abby gripped Jeri's hand till her knuckles cracked. Jumbled voices, questions, sounds of alarm, and discussion rose in a mighty crescendo throughout the room.

"Girls! Girls!" Head Long clinked her glass so hard Jeri thought it would surely shatter. A fine mist of sweat glistened on her forehead. "Do not panic! Rescue workers are searching for the van. We know they entered the Two-Mile Stretch at the other end."

Jeri turned to Abby. "What does that mean? They didn't come out?"

The Stretch was a curvy, deserted, two-mile section of Highway 6 just outside the town of Landmark Hills. The highway meandered along Landmark Mountain on one side and Sutter Lake on the other side. A gas station-convenience store marked one end of the Stretch, but there were no other buildings for two miles, until you passed Dale's Diner in Landmark Hills. The Landmark School for Girls was located up a scenic winding road from the town, and many of its stately buildings could be seen from Main Street.

The headmistress buttoned and unbuttoned her gray suit jacket. "Apparently the van did not emerge on the Landmark Hills end of the Stretch," she added.

Jeri raised her hand. The headmistress peered over her half-glasses and nodded.

"If they entered the Stretch," Jeri asked, "but didn't come out, does that mean the van went into the lake?"

Girls all around Jeri gasped. It felt as if the dining hall itself was holding its breath. The headmistress's eyes shot daggers. "That's *not* what I'm saying. We haven't yet located the van, that's all. A search is underway already, and the girls and Mr. Reeves will no doubt turn up, safe and sound." She paused. "If your parents happen to call, reassure them that it's just a mix-up. Do you understand?"

Jeri frowned. How could they reassure their parents when they didn't know it *was* a mix-up? Across from Jeri, Nikki stared at her hands, palms down on the white tablecloth. Tears welled up in Abby's frightened eyes.

Jeri raised her hand again. "My roommate, Rosa Sanchez, was on the trip," she said. "Can I go help search?"

"I understand your desire, but no," The Head said. "Police and other adult rescue workers are on the scene. Children are not allowed."

Voices rose and fell and rose again, waves of frightened questions rippling through the dining hall. Ms. Carter stood up at the teachers' table. "Ms. Long, could you tell us exactly who is missing?"

The headmistress nodded briefly. "Quiet down, girls. To answer Ms. Carter's question, there were six girls in the van with Mr. Reeves. Mostly they're art and drama students: Rosa Sanchez and Heather Langley, both sixth graders. A seventh grader, Lisa Poole. Sarah Callahan, an eighth grader." Cries arose from several tables, and the headmistress raised her voice. "And two ninth graders, Savanah Stone and Hilary Lyttle."

"Thank you," Ms. Carter said, sitting down. Jeri

wondered if she was relieved that only one girl was from Hampton House.

Jeri stood again. "If we can't help search for our friends, could we just go down to the Stretch and wait?" She paused. "Please? We just want to be there when they're found."

Without answering, the headmistress walked on rubber-soled shoes over to the dining hall's floor-to-ceiling windows. The center panes were French windows that opened out onto a balcony. The headmistress, framed by velvet drapes held open with gold cords, gazed over the campus. For one very brief second, her shoulders drooped. When she turned back to the girls, though, her posture was military: shoulders back, chin down, and expression sober.

"The temperature is dropping. If you want to wait at the Stretch, bundle up in extra layers. Stay with your house mothers and gather out front in ten minutes."

Chairs scraped back, and linen napkins fell to the floor as girls raced to their dorm rooms for extra hats, boots, and mittens. Jeri pulled on two pairs of socks and then stuck her feet in plastic bags before jamming them into her soggy snow boots.

A knock sounded on the door, and Abby opened it a few inches. "You ready?"

"Ready." Jeri glanced at Rosa's empty bed before following Abby out and pulling the door closed. *Please, God, let Rosa and the others be all right!*

The girls and house mothers were transported down the hill to the search site in several of the teachers' cars. The ride seemed unreal, as if time had stopped. Jeri kept expecting someone to say there'd been a terrible mistake, that Rosa was fine. Judging by the pale faces of the other girls, they were also in shock—and too frightened to put their fears into words. Were their friends at the bottom of the lake? Or had there been a crash and they were pinned inside the van? Or were they thrown from the vehicle and wandering, dazed and injured, in the woods by the lake? Or maybe a serial killer was loose and they'd all been—

That's enough! Jeri shook herself. *Stop it!*

She reminded herself that Rosa and the other missing girls were with Mr. Reeves. He might be almost forty, but he was stocky and muscular, as solid-looking as a block of wood. She'd seen him carry a marble statue into class by himself one day. He was strong enough to take care of Rosa and the others. He'd get them home safely. She had to believe that.

By the time they arrived at the Two-Mile Stretch, a crowd had gathered. Stunned townspeople, four doctors and nurses, and half a dozen police officers milled around. An ambulance was parked near two police cars, its lights and siren off.

One officer, his nose and ears bright red, shouted through a bullhorn. "Attention, folks!" His booming voice bounced against the mountainside and echoed back.

Jeri stamped her cold feet and stuck her fists in her pockets. Nikki stood to her left, her hands tucked in her armpits. Abby shrank inside her short coat while the wind whipped blonde strands across her eyes.

"I'm Police Chief Reynolds. Here's the situation." With his square face, angular jaw, and heavy neck, the police officer reminded Jeri of a granite sculpture. "Hal at the Gas-U-Up saw the school van enter the Two-Mile Stretch at 4:30, after filling up at his station. The vehicle—a nine-passenger Suburban—was not seen coming out the other end. A man at Dale's Diner was waiting there for someone and watching the road the whole time. The SUV never showed up. No one else in town saw it pass down Main Street, and many were on the sidewalk at that hour."

Nikki nudged Jeri, who lost her balance. "You couldn't miss the van either, not in those ugly school colors."

Jeri agreed. Their school van was bright purple with Landmark School painted in orange letters on the side.

"The temperature's dropping," the police chief shouted, "so listen up. Both ends of the Stretch are roadblocked. A drive through earlier showed that the guardrail along the lake isn't dented anywhere. We're sure the vehicle didn't break through it and go into the lake."

Abby clapped her mittened hands. "That's good!"

"However," he continued, "no roads head up the mountain, and the van had to go somewhere."

A man behind Jeri yelled out, "Keith might've gassed up and then turned around and drove off somewhere else."

"I was coming to that." In the frosty air, the policeman's breath made a white cloud around his head. "We have a witness who saw them halfway through the Stretch."

"That's right." Mrs. Wilson, Landmark's nutrition teacher, stepped forward. Her stiffly sprayed hair combed out to one side never moved, even in the strong wind. "I was in the middle of the Stretch going the other way, and I passed the van. Keith Reeves waved at me."

The officer ticked off the places they couldn't be. "They didn't come out of the Stretch into town. The van couldn't drive straight up the mountainside. There aren't any roads there. It didn't plunge through the guardrail. One possibility is that they went into the lake using the fishing access road near the end of the Stretch. We'll check that out first."

Jeri studied the frozen lake, gray with sinister shadows, visible only as far as headlights and flashlights reached. Dead weeds and thick brush, as well as leafless river birch and willows, hid the shoreline from view. What horrible secret was hidden beneath its surface? Jeri shuddered at the idea of Rosa and the others trapped in that icy, watery grave.

Stop it! she ordered herself.

"Split into two groups," the police officer said. "Half of you start at each end of the guardrail. Go down to the lakeshore and walk toward each other till you meet in the middle. Look for tire tracks, breaks in the ice, broken brush. Also look for evidence that might indicate Keith drove off into the woods around the lake." He paused. "He could have suffered a heart attack or stroke and gone into the lake. We just don't know. It's impossible for a van to just disappear along this stretch. The sooner we find it, the better for all involved. Move quickly, but carefully."

Jeri followed the woman beside her to the end of the guardrail. Sharp rocks jabbed through her snow boots. Icy wind pounded her forehead as she trudged along, and she pulled her stocking cap lower and scarf higher. She plowed through snow and tangled brush down to Sutter Lake.

"Sorry, young lady." A police officer stepped in front of Jeri. "Weren't you told to stay back behind the orange tape?"

Jeri saw the headmistress coming. "I'm sorry. I forgot. I'm just so worried. My roommate is in that van."

"Jeri!" Head Long's voice was sharp in the freezing night air. "I told you—"

"I'm coming."

The officer nodded at the headmistress. "Ma'am, keep your students under control, or they need to leave. We can't babysit them for you."

Jeri was stunned. Nobody talked to The Head that way! The headmistress nodded curtly, looked like she wanted to turn the officer over her knee, and clutched Jeri's arm. "Go back to your friends," she said through gritted teeth.

Frozen muddy ruts were glazed with ice, and Jeri fell, biting her tongue. She tasted blood, but barely noticed it as she watched the searchers move slowly along the shoreline. In twenty minutes her toes were numb. If *she* were cold, Jeri shuddered to think how Rosa probably felt.

Abby's teeth chattered, making her chin quiver. Jeri untied her scarf. "Here, take this."

"N-no, I'm okay."

"Abby, you're freezing. Take it."

"Thanks, Jer." Although Abby wore jeans, her short jacket wasn't enough protection against the frigid wind whipping across the lake.

Jeri hunched down inside her collar, grateful now for the full-length, down-filled coat her mom had insisted on buying. The raw wind made her eyes water; and tears dripping down her cheeks froze halfway.

She stomped her freezing feet while her mind replayed Rosa mini-movies: Rosa throwing Cheerios at her at breakfast, Rosa sending her a singing hyena e-card, and Rosa whispering after lights-out while her flashlight beam played across the ceiling.

Toward the west, Jeri spotted one group approaching from around a bend. Within ten minutes, both groups met in the middle. Jeri ran to the guardrail and yelled to a man in green coveralls. "Did you find anything?"

His breath came out in puffs of white vapor. "No. Nothing."

Behind her, Nikki stomped her feet. Abby cried without making a sound. Jeri shuddered as the wind changed from bitter to bone-chilling.

A man in a furry parka standing next to Jeri was joined by a bearded man from the search party. "The van didn't go in the lake. I'll stake my life on it."

"It had to go somewhere." The man in a tan coat brushed at the frost accumulating in his beard. "Maybe taking off is Keith's idea of a practical joke."

"No!" Jeri burst out. The men turned to gawk at her. "I know Mr. Reeves. He'd never do something like that."

"Well, honey, they've disappeared." The bearded man leaned close to her face. "What do you think happened? Little green aliens in UFOs?"

"That's not funny," Jeri said. "My roommate is missing."

The man looked embarrassed. "Sorry," he said. "Could be carjacking. Lot of that these days."

Jeri frowned. "Huh?"

"Where a thief takes the vehicle, but leaves the people miles and miles away so they can't get to help till the carjacker gets away." The bearded man jammed his hands in his pants pockets. "Cold night to be wandering in the dark."

The man in the parka patted Jeri's arm. "Don't worry. Maybe they went for a bite to eat before coming back to school, and they didn't tell anyone."

Jeri shook her head. "Our headmistress has to give permission for stuff like that. She doesn't know where they are either."

Ms. Carter tapped her on the shoulder. "We need to go now and get thawed out."

Jeri spun around. "Not yet!"

"We'll come back tomorrow, when it's light." Mouth trembling, Ms. Carter pulled her close for a moment. "There's nothing we can do here tonight."

Rosa, where are you? Jeri wanted to scream. They followed the house mother back to the cars parked at the roadblock. Huddled in their coats, it was a silent trip back up the hill to the school. Jeri stared out the window. The moon's light reflected off the snowy hillside. At any other time, the scene would inspire peace. Not tonight. Her best friend was out there—somewhere—frightened and maybe hurt.

Oh, Lord, I'm sorry for being mad at Rosa this afternoon. Please keep them all safe.

If only there was something she could do. She'd never felt so helpless in her life.

It took Jeri a good hour sitting by her radiator to warm up. How cold Rosa must be! How terrified! Her thoughts were interrupted by the phone. She glanced at the clock—9:34—as she grabbed it. "Hello?"

"Rosa?"

"No, it's Jeri."

"Sí! How are you?"

"Mrs. Sanchez?" The connection to South America was surprisingly clear. "I'm fine." Jeri cringed at the lie.

"Good! I hope Rosa is behaving." She laughed. "May I speak to her?"

"Well ..." Jeri recalled the headmistress's warning at suppertime. "She's not here right now. Can I take a message?"

"Is she studying, or is that too much to hope for?"

"That's too much to hope for."

"When should I call back?" asked Mrs. Sanchez.

Jeri felt trapped, remembering The Head's official keep-quiet order. But didn't Rosa's parents have a right to know their daughter was missing? She just couldn't lie to them.

"Mrs. Sanchez, something's happened," she said. "I think you should call the headmistress."

"Why? What's going on?"

Jeri felt panic rising within her. She wasn't supposed to tell! And she didn't really know anything.

"Jeri? What's happened to Rosa? What?"

"I'm sure they'll find everybody soon. Please don't worry."

"Find who?" Rosa's mother demanded. "What are you talking about?"

"Please talk to the headmistress," pleaded Jeri.

"But I'm talking to *you*. Jeri, *please* tell me what's happened!"

Jeri would have given anything to spare them this news. She took a deep breath. "The school van she was riding in has … well … disappeared." She heard a gasp on the other end. "They were on their way back to school after a field trip. At first the police thought the van went into the lake, but a rescue crew searched around it. They didn't find any breaks in the ice. So that's good."

Rosa's mom whispered something that sounded like a prayer. "Is there—? I mean, has there—?" She gulped. "Are the police saying they were kidnapped? Has there been a ransom note?"

"No, of course not," Jeri said, her heart suddenly pounding. She hadn't thought about them being kidnapped!

"Why weren't we called? Maybe they couldn't reach us down here."

"I don't know, Mrs. Sanchez. Please call the headmistress. She might have more news by now." *And I'm in hot water the minute Head Long hears what I told Rosa's mother.* Jeri swallowed the lump in her throat.

Jeri hung up, but couldn't move for a full minute. She could only imagine the horror of Rosa's parents dealing with this news halfway around the world.

As if in a trance, she stared at the top of Rosa's desk. There were three diet books there, collecting dust. Rosa had bought them after putting on fifteen pounds their first semester. But it was the photos she couldn't take her eyes from.

Lining them up, Jeri studied the pictures taken with Rosa: making popcorn balls down in the kitchen, decorating a tiny Christmas tree in their bedroom, riding the Tilt-a-Whirl at the fair, Jeri braiding Rosa's waist-length hair, and more. Each snapshot was a memory.

They had to find Rosa soon. Jeri couldn't just go to bed while Rosa was out there, freezing and maybe injured. She had to do something now. *Tonight*!

But what?

3
FEELING HELPLESS

Thursday, 10:06 p.m. to Friday, 11:40 a.m.

The phone jangled, interrupting Jeri's desperate thoughts. "Hello?"

"Jeri? It's Mom. I got your email when I got back to the motel."

"Mom, I'm so glad you called! It's horrible! I can't believe it! It's—"

"Honey, settle down." Her mom's voice was soothing. "Even though I can't make it for Parents' Weekend, hopefully within six weeks—"

"Rosa's missing!" Jeri cried.

"*What?*"

"She was in the school van. The police thought it went into the lake—"

"Oh Jeri!"

"—but they searched around the lake by the highway, and there's no place where the ice is broken or anything." She gasped for breath.

"Oh, honey, I'm so sorry." Mom paused. "Let's pray."

Jeri listened, and her mom's words soothed her panicky heart. She prayed for a hedge of protection around the missing girls, guidance for the rescue team, and peace for all involved. She also reminded Jeri that God was in control. "Remember, he knows where they are—they aren't lost to *him*—and he's with them."

"But what if they've been kidnapped?" asked Jeri.

"There's no evidence of that, is there?"

"No, I guess not. I'm so scared, Mom."

"I know. It comes from feeling helpless," Mom said. "When that feeling hits you, remember to pray. That will make the most difference, for you *and* for Rosa. Now you need to go to bed and—"

"I could never sleep!"

"At least lie down and rest. You'll need lots of energy tomorrow."

After saying their good-byes, Jeri changed into flannel pajamas, but the wind whistling through the gap by the windowsill chilled her. If she was cold, how much more must Rosa be!

To feel less alone, she set the photo of herself and Mom on her bedside table, left her night-light on, and crawled into bed. She couldn't pray except to say, *Help Rosa. Please find Rosa.*

Jeri stared at the photo taken in their porch swing. Her mom's blonde curls and dainty features contrasted sharply with Jeri's stick-straight brown hair and large front teeth. But she and Mom were definitely related.

Kids usually figured Jeri was named after her dad. Instead, she was named for the city of Jericho in the Bible. "The doctors said I shouldn't be having a baby," her mom had said. "My heart and kidneys couldn't handle it. I was advised to end the pregnancy, but you were a gift from God, and we wanted you so much. I was petrified, but no matter how sick I got, no matter how *scared* I got, I was determined to carry you as long as possible."

It had been touch and go, Jeri knew. During the scary times, her mom loved to read about Joshua fighting the battle of Jericho.

Jeri knew the story by heart. Jericho was a walled city. God's battle plan for Joshua was extremely odd. "Your armed men should march around the city once per day for six days. Seven priests shall carry trumpets. On the seventh day, march around the city seven times, with the priests blowing the trumpets. Then have the whole army shout! The city walls will collapse and the army will go straight in."

Those instructions must have been hard to obey. But by trusting God's plan—even when it didn't make sense—Joshua was given the victory. Her mom had been in a battle too—for both their lives. So when Jeri was born, fat and sassy, she was named Jericho.

If only her mom could be here now, Jeri thought. Rolling on her side, she was tempted to check her email. When she was alone, email connected her to the outside world. She didn't even mind getting spam.

Say, what about *sending* a mass email? She could put out an alert about the missing girls! Then people in the area could be on the lookout for the van. She'd ask people to pray too. Mom said you could never have too many people praying. Jeri threw back her covers and snapped on her desk lamp. Wiggling the mouse, she brought her computer screen to life.

With lips pressed together, she worked to create an attention-getting "alert." First, she scanned a photo of Rosa into her computer. She listed her name, size, weight, hair color, and how she was dressed that morning. Next came a description of the school van, plus when and where it was last seen. She sent the mass email alert to everyone in her address book, even Mom in Iowa. She knew Mom would forward it to her church's prayer chain and all her friends.

After clicking "send," Jeri's gaze rested on the scraps of paper that were Rosa's unfinished advice column. Just that afternoon Jeri'd wished for something *big* to report on—but not this! If only she really had the skills—and the courage—to investigate.

Wait. What about that reporter, Jake Philips? He'd been successful in solving crimes, and he'd left his business card with her after visiting her class. Jeri rummaged in her drawer and finally found it. As she studied the card, she recalled The Head's words about keeping quiet. Would she get in trouble for calling Jake? Surely not. The police would have contacted the media already anyway, but would they think to call an *investigative* reporter? That's what they really needed. With shaking fingers, she dialed his cell phone number.

"Jake Philips? You probably don't remember me." She gulped. "I'm Jeri McKane. You spoke to my class at Landmark School last fall."

"Sure. You wanted to be a reporter."

"Yes!" Jeri was flattered that he remembered. "I know it's late, but something awful happened here tonight. We need a reporter right away who can dig into things." She told him about the missing girls and the search so far. "Could you come over tonight?"

"Let me check with my boss," he said. "If he okays it, I'll be on the road in half an hour. But I don't live near Landmark Hills anymore. I got a promotion at Christmas. Now I live in Connors, so I'm six hours away. If I start soon, I could be there by five in the morning."

"You'll come? Thank you!"

"Thanks for the tip, Jeri. Aren't there news crews there already?"

"No, at least not when we were down there. Just police and some rescue people."

"I'll get there by morning and start nosing around." He said something to someone in the background and then added, "Try not to worry. And thanks for calling me. See you tomorrow."

Jeri sat slumped in her chair until her shivering roused her. It was past 1:00 a.m. She ought to get in bed, but she couldn't settle down. Maybe Abby was still awake and could talk to her.

She opened the door into the dark, cavernous hallway. Back pressed against the wall, Jeri inched along toward Abby's room. She stretched her arm to the right as her fingers searched for the next bedroom door. She'd knock softly and hope Abby heard her. Step-by-step, Jeri blindly slid her arm along the wall. Just then she touched something warm—a human hand!

Jeri jerked back as if scorched and smothered a shriek. Her heart and head thumped wildly. "Who's there?" she croaked.

"J-Jeri?" Abby stammered.

"Abby? Come over to my room."

The two girls tiptoed back down the hall. Jeri shut

the door before turning on the bedside lamp. "Man, you made me flip out!"

"What about *me*?" Abby said. "I touch the wall and find fingers!" She twisted a strand of hair around and around. "I didn't feel like being by myself."

"Where's Nikki?"

"Sound asleep, snoring like an old man. How can she sleep at a time like this?" Abby shivered. "I knew you'd be up."

"Rosa wouldn't care if you slept in her bed. Crawl in."

Abby pushed aside the stuffed monkey and elephant and slipped between Rosa's leopard-print sheets. Jeri crawled under her own covers and told her about Mrs. Sanchez's phone call.

"I feel bad for her parents," Abby said. "I know it would kill my mom."

"I just wish I had something to tell them. Maybe we'll have good news soon." Jeri told her about the email alert she'd sent out.

"Great idea!" Abby rubbed her red nose. "Did you call your mom? She might see it on the news and be scared."

"She called earlier about something else." Suddenly, missing Parents' Weekend didn't sound like much of a tragedy. "I told her about Rosa and the others. Talking to her really helped."

"What did she say?" Abby asked, already sounding a bit drowsy.

"She reminded me that God's in control, and that *he* knows where they all are. They aren't lost to him."

Abby bit her lip. "I hope Rosa knows that."

Jeri hoped so too.

At 6:30 Friday morning Jeri was awakened by the house mother out in the hall. "Up, girls, and dress warmly! Friday's classes are cancelled. We've been asked to supply hot food and drinks for the search parties." Ms. Carter knocked on Jeri's door and opened it. "The police also want you to bring along a piece of clothing Rosa's worn—something that hasn't been washed yet. They're collecting clothing belonging to each missing girl."

Jeri rubbed her eyes. "Okay, but what for?"

The house mother's voice was a husky whisper. "The dogs need something to sniff to help find Rosa."

"Oh." *To find Rosa or to find Rosa's body?*

Jeri struggled to a sitting position and shook her head to clear it. Pale light oozed in around the edges of the drapes. Abby was already gone, and Rosa's giraffe-print bedspread was smooth. Jeri dressed fast and then joined the other sixth graders for a hot oatmeal breakfast in the kitchen. Then she bagged up two of Rosa's dirty socks and a knit hat for the dogs to sniff.

Within half an hour, the Hampton House girls were at the Two-Mile Stretch, handing out warm rolls and coffee and hot cider supplied by the dining hall. Jeri and Abby worked as a team, moving among the crowd with their paper sacks and Styrofoam cups.

Jeri thought the frozen lake looked sinister now. How had Rosa spent the night? Had she even woken up this morning? Jeri stared up at the top of snowcapped Landmark Mountain, comforted by how it towered protectively over the town, their school, and the lake. Tall armies of white pine stood at attention on every slope of the mountain, guarding the picturesque town. A V-formation of honking Canada geese flew north overhead, knowing instinctively that spring and new life were just around the corner.

A chill passed through Jeri. *Would Rosa be around for that?*

After handing out her last rolls, Jeri searched the area for Jake Philips. Finally, on the other side of the fire truck she spotted a white van with a satellite dish on top. Yes! He'd made it! Odd, though, that there weren't any other news crews. Surely the school and police weren't keeping it secret. In any case, thanks to her quick thinking, Jake and some purple-haired camera girl were already there.

Jeri glanced behind her where the police were organizing the milling crowd into search parties. She spotted Houston, their stable hand, with a knot of men and several teachers.

Beyond them were some boys from a private school in nearby Rock River. One was Jonathan Fielding, a tall, thin boy who went to Landmark Hills Community Church and was in Jeri's Sunday school class. His huge ears had already turned bright red from the cold.

She hoped that—with everyone working together—the van would be found soon. She pushed through the crowd to greet the reporter.Jake. He looked the same, with his light brown hair sticking up in a cowlick and dazzling white teeth too perfect to be real. She listened as he reported about the missing students. Now everyone in the surrounding towns and states could be on the lookout.

"Stop that camera!" an angry voice shouted. "Immediately!"

Jeri jumped aside as The Head charged at Jake, waving her arms. The camera kept rolling as they argued. Then the headmistress turned in Jeri's direction, lips pressed in a hard, thin line.

"He tells me," she said, clipping her words, "that you're responsible for him being here."

Jeri nodded in confusion. Didn't she deserve a pat on the back for her quick thinking? "I called him last night."

The Head's perfect skin was marred by angry splotches. "Yes, and the camera was rolling even before I arrived this morning."

"But isn't that a good thing?" Jeri asked.

"No!" she exploded. "No, it's not," she repeated at a lower decibel. "I specifically wanted the media kept *out!*"

"But ... but why?"

"It will damage the school's reputation." She spoke through clenched jaws. "What parents want to send their child somewhere to get lost or kidnapped or drowned?"

Jeri flinched as if struck.

The headmistress stared through Jeri as if she were a pane of glass. "Never take matters into your own hands again! Do you understand me?"

Jeri nodded. Then, with a sinking feeling, she remembered her email alert. Heaven only knew how far her message had traveled by now.

The sight of two more news crews showing up distracted the headmistress, who hurried off. Jeri was crushed. She thought she'd done such a helpful thing by contacting Jake. It had sounded brilliant when it popped into her head.

Apparently the headmistress didn't think so.

The next hour seemed to last an eternity while they waited for news from the search and rescue teams. The wind coming across the lake was bitter cold and cut through coats, jeans, hats, and mittens. After passing out all her warm food and coffee, Jeri held a cup of cider up to her face, letting the steam warm her nose and melt the ice droplets from her eyelashes. Voices of curious onlookers drifted around her.

"If they didn't go into the lake, then it has to be an abduction," one lady in a leather coat said. "Who else but Keith Reeves could have done it?"

Her friend agreed. "They're expecting a ransom note from him at any time."

Jeri couldn't believe what she'd just heard. She knew Mr. Reeves really well. He'd been very kind to her last Thanksgiving. When she couldn't go home for the holiday, he'd taken her and Rosa to his house for dinner with his elderly mother. Jeri had eaten pumpkin pie till she was more stuffed than the Butterball turkey. Afterward, all four of them played Parcheesi by the fireplace. No way could Mr. Reeves do something as horrendous as kidnap someone! She turned to the two ladies.

"Excuse me, but I know Mr. Reeves," Jeri said. "He'd never kidnap anybody."

"Sweetie," the first woman said, "the van was driven somewhere. He was the only person who could drive."

"If they've been kidnapped, it wasn't by Mr. Reeves," Jeri said. "Maybe a stranger attacked him and got the van's keys and drove away with the girls."

"I guess that's possible," the second woman said, "but somebody said he has gambling debts from hanging out at casinos. Now he can write six ransom notes and make a killing."

"Dorothy!"

"Sorry. Poor choice of words." The woman looked embarrassed. "Still, he's the most likely suspect. One girl's parents said they'd pay *anything* to get their daughter back."

Jeri felt sick at their gossipy accusations. "Who are the parents?"

The one named Dorothy pointed. "See that couple in matching black coats? The guy with the black mustache? They're Heather Langley's parents."

Heather—the other sixth grader on the trip—lived in a different dorm. Jeri headed toward the parents. If *her* terrified mom was waiting in the freezing cold for some news, she hoped all kinds of people—even strangers—would try to comfort her.

"Mr. and Mrs. Langley?" The couple turned around. Up close, Mr. Langley's short clipped mustache looked more like dirty toothbrush bristles. And Mrs. Langley smelled sooty, like she smoked too much. "I'm Jeri McKane, and Heather's in my class. I'm sorry about what's happened."

"Thank you, dear," the stick-thin woman said, holding out her slender hand.

Jeri took off her mitten and shook it. The woman's fingers were cool and smooth. It was like shaking hands with a rubber glove.

Mr. Langley, however, looked more like a mean, hungry dog. "They'll be found soon," he snarled, "but only after a ransom is paid." His voice rose, and people turned to stare. "And guess who will have to pay the ransom for the girls too poor to pay? People like me!"

"Lance, please!" his wife begged.

The man's words popped out like ice cubes, hard and cold. "Two of the missing kids are scholarship students. *Their* families can't pay any ransom. So guess who has to pay their share?"

Heather's mom stared at the frozen ground, her face pinched and red.

"Listen to me!" A tiny birdlike woman picked her way toward them. "My Sarah's on that van. She's a scholarship student, but I don't need you to pay anything!"

Mr. Langley nailed her with a steely glare. "Whose gifts already support your daughter's education? I donate the money for *three* scholarships."

"Did it ever occur to you that *you're* at fault?" Sarah's mom asked, a sob in her voice. "My child got abducted for a ransom only because she had the rotten luck to be on the van with your spoiled *rich* kid!"

"How dare you!" the man spluttered.

"Please stop!" Jeri said. "It's nobody's fault."

"Who asked you?" Mr. Langley snarled.

Jeri jerked back. "If you'd just calm down —"

"Easy for you to say!" Sarah's mom said.

Jeri stumbled backward. Why was she getting attacked from both sides? She only wanted to help the parents feel better. And why was The Head so furious about Jake? If she wanted the van found, she should be thrilled that Jake got the word out early to everyone in the state—even the country. Why try to hush it up?

No matter how Jeri looked at it, nothing added up.

4

SUSPICIONS

Friday, 11:41 a.m. to 1:05 p.m.

After the searchers returned from the other side of the lake—still clueless—the girls went back to school for lunch. They filed into the dining hall in silence, as if they were at a funeral. Little was said as they were served their hot beef stew.

The Head stepped to a microphone. "Before you eat, I want to thank each of you for your efforts this morning. So many rescue workers expressed their gratitude for your warm food and drink." She paused. "Our kitchen staff is now preparing more refreshments for after lunch. I understand that there's less ground to cover this afternoon, so not as many of you will be needed. However, since the teachers and house mothers want to continue to help in the search, students who don't serve refreshments will be confined to their dorms for the remainder of the day."

Jeri glanced at Abby and Nikki, who both nodded. Jeri agreed. She was going back to help too.

"One other thing—" The Head's cell phone rang. She flipped it open and turned her back to the girls.

No one moved or whispered. It was so quiet Jeri could hear the cooks in the kitchen talking.

The Head smiled as she stepped back to the mike. "We've had a breakthrough! Heather's parents received a ransom note through email. Heather's family intends to pay it immediately. We could have the students back by supper time!"

Thank you, Lord! Oh, thank you! Jeri gripped her hands together. Maybe the nightmare *would* be over soon.

"The search will continue, however, until everyone is back, safe and sound," the headmistress said.

Jeri thought that was smart. She'd read how kidnappers sometimes tried to get money without giving the kids back. She'd seen a movie where they tried to collect when the kids were no longer even alive.

No! Don't even think that.

By the time Jeri finished lunch, she'd decided to go see Mr. Reeves's mother while Nikki and Abby handed out refreshments. His mother was old, and without her son there, maybe she needed something. Hopefully The Head was right, and the ransom money would get the girls and Mr. Reeves released soon. The girls would be safe, and Mr. Reeves would no longer be suspected.

Back in her room, Jeri changed into dry clothes and grabbed a notebook and pen. At the last minute, she stuck a voice-activated tape recorder from the media center in her coat pocket. Soon she was biking down the long slope from the school to town.

Once there, she biked two blocks past the diner, then turned off Main Street onto Rolling Hills Lane. If her memory was right, the Reeves's light blue cottage was four houses down. When she pulled into their driveway, she noticed the drawn curtains in the living room twitch and then fall closed again.

Before she could ring the bell, Mrs. Reeves opened the front door and squinted into the bright winter sunshine. She was more stooped than Jeri remembered, but the tight gray curls and sharp blue eyes were the same. Except now her eyes were red-rimmed. Dimpled arms peeked out from a shapeless olive green muumuu. It was printed with palm trees and parrots in hot pink and turquoise.

"Mrs. Reeves? Do you remember me? Jeri McKane?"

Mrs. Reeves leaned forward and squinted harder. Then a smile creased her face. "Of course. You and your friend ate a whole pumpkin pie."

Jeri laughed at the exaggeration—although she wasn't far off. "Can I talk to you? About Mr. Reeves?"

The older lady unlatched the screen door and opened it, giving Jeri a better look at her face. She'd obviously been crying. A lot. Jeri stepped into the living room, and it looked exactly as it had at Thanksgiving, minus the construction paper decorations. Ceramic cardinals and blue jays sat on the window ledge, a pile of *TV Guide* magazines were stacked by a rocker, and doilies were draped on the backs of chairs and armrests.

"I was just having my coffee. How about a glass of milk? Or hot chocolate?"

"No, thanks."

Mrs. Reeves offered Jeri a cookie for her sweet tooth, then settled into her glider rocker. The chair creaked under her weight. "What did you want to ask me?"

"I'm sorry to bother you. I suppose you've been swamped with people stopping by."

"Hardly." Her voice sounded both distressed and con-fused. "It's like I suddenly have leprosy. I guess people don't want to be associated with me." A sob caught in her throat, and she burst out, "Don't they *understand*? I'm terrified, just like them. *My* child is missing too!" She jerked and spilled some coffee on her muumuu. Jeri didn't know what to say. "My son would never hurt anyone, especially not a child. How can they say such things? How?" Tears rolled down her face, following the lines and wrinkles till they dripped off her chin.

"I know how you feel, sort of." Jeri hunched her shoulders. "Rosa's missing too."

"I can promise you that Keith did *not* take her."

"I never thought he did." Jeri moved to sit on the floor by the rocker. "They'll find Mr. Reeves. Lots of people don't think he's guilty. Mom says people don't know what to say, so they stay away and don't say anything."

Mrs. Reeves gazed at the pair of mountain paintings over the couch. "I've been sitting in this chair looking at Keith's watercolors since five this morning. I was awake thinking all night." She gripped Jeri's hand. "I remembered things."

"Like what?"

"Troublesome things."

"Like what?" Jeri squeezed her hand gently.

"Keith has taken care of me all his life, ever since his daddy died. Keith was only twelve." She set her coffee cup on an end table.

"He sounds like a wonderful son."

"He is! He is!" She leaned close to Jeri and whispered, as if she thought there were spies lurking behind the chair. "Keith's been acting odd lately."

Jeri tensed. "Odd how?"

"Secretive."

Jeri nodded for her to continue and then finally asked, "Secretive how?"

"He goes out at night and doesn't say where. He says he wants to be alone." Her eyes grew round and frightened. "What if he has some terminal disease? I think he's secretly seeing doctors and doesn't want to worry me."

Jeri hoped her thoughts didn't show on her face. Did this sweet woman really think her son was seeing *doctors* at night? What *was* Mr. Reeves up to? Could those women on the bridge be right about him visiting gambling casinos? Of course, Mrs. Reeves might be right. If her son *was* really sick, he might need expensive treatments or medicine. He might need to make some big money fast—either by gambling or collecting a ransom.

"Have you seen the TV news?" Mrs. Reeves asked.

"No." Jeri wondered if she knew about the ransom note yet. "I've been at the Stretch giving out hot drinks and food to the rescue workers."

"The coverage has been too horrible for words. That young reporter who belongs in a toothpaste commercial keeps blaming Keith. He might as well cut my heart out."

Jeri wanted to sink into the floor. That had to be Jake. "I'm sorry, but I'm the reason he's here. I called him."

"What!"

"He doesn't just report the news, he investigates things. I wanted him to get the word out fast so people would be watching for the van." Jeri sighed. "The headmistress didn't see it that way, though. She yelled at me in front of a bunch of people."

"*Humph*. That woman is *not* my favorite person."

Jeri's eyes widened in surprise. "You know her?"

"I know *about* her. From Keith." She shook her head. "Before Christmas, Keith told her the van should be replaced. Several things were wrong with it—bad brakes, something called a drive shaft, things like that. He was afraid the brakes would give out sometime and he'd go over the side of the mountain with a load of kids."

"What did she do?"

"She ignored him, but he filed a report with someone. He didn't want to be held responsible if there was trouble."

Jeri was shocked. Absentmindedly, she patted her coat pocket, glad that the recorder was taping. This was important information. Before she could ask more questions, a sharp rap sounded on the door. "I'll get it," Jeri said.

Two uniformed policemen stood on the steps. Her heart skipped a beat. "Have you found Mr. Reeves and the girls?" she asked, holding her breath.

The younger officer shook his head. "No. Sorry." He paused. "Is Mrs. Reeves in?"

Jeri let them both in. They stood, hats in hand, in front of Mrs. Reeves. "Ma'am, we're sorry, but we need to ask you some questions. There's been a ransom note."

Mrs. Reeves glared at them, gripping the chair arms as if bracing herself. "I assume you want to know if it's Keith's handwriting."

"No, the note was typed. It's an email." The older policeman squatted down next to Mrs. Reeves's chair. "I hate to ask this, but do you know where your son is?"

"Of course not." Mrs. Reeves blinked at him, clearly confused. "I have to find out things on TV, like everyone else."

He cleared his throat. "I'm sorry, Ma'am, I'm asking if you're hiding your son ... or if you know where he's hiding."

"He's not hiding!" Tears welled up in her eyes. "I have no idea where he is."

"Has he asked you for money lately? A loan maybe?"

"No, never. He's a good money manager. Has been since he was a small boy."

"Have you two been getting along lately?" the older policeman asked.

She looked puzzled. "Of course. He's such a good son. I don't know what I'd do without him."

"Yes, Ma'am, I understand that, but ..."

"But what?" Jeri asked.

"Well, there's been talk," the older officer said. "People are saying he was tired of caring for his mother, that he wanted to start a new life somewhere else. He'd need a chunk of money to do that."

Mrs. Reeves looked as if she'd been pierced through the heart. "Tired of me?" she asked, her voice thin and wavery.

Jeri's heart sank. Earlier Mrs. Reeves had said her son wanted to be alone a lot. *Was* he tired of taking care of her? *Oh, Lord, please don't let that be true.*

After the officers drove away, Jeri took Mrs. Reeves's coffee cup to the kitchen for a refill. She hoped a jolt of caffeine would shake the older woman out of her frozen state. She hadn't moved a muscle since they left. The tiny kitchen was cluttered, with half a dozen small appliances and many prescription bottles covering the countertops. Jeri poured the last cup of coffee and rinsed the pot under the leaky kitchen faucet.

She stepped on the pedal of the flip-lid wastebasket and tossed the paper napkins in. A document caught her eye, and she pulled it out. It was a bank statement bearing Mr. Reeves's name and address. She tried to make sense of the rows of figures. It was hard, but one thing was crystal clear.

Just two days before the van's disappearance, Mr. Reeves had withdrawn nearly every penny he had in his savings account.

With a sinking feeling, she folded the paper and tucked it into her pocket. Then she took Mrs. Reeves her fresh coffee, covered her with an afghan, hugged her, and left.

Pedaling back to Main Street, Jeri considered Mr. Reeves's bank statement. He'd withdrawn several thousand dollars a few days ago. For what? Were the police right that he'd been planning to leave town? Did he need even more money to make a new life somewhere else? Like a chunk he could get from a ransom note?

After turning the corner, Jeri biked two blocks to Dale's Diner. She was surprised to see Nikki coming out of the front door. "What's up?" Jeri asked.

"Getting warmed up." Nikki patted her stomach. "I ate again too—hamburger and onion rings and cherry pie. That stew for lunch was pathetic."

Jeri wished she had that kind of extra cash lying around. The three dollars in her pocket wouldn't buy much.

"You're crazy, biking when it's so cold," said Nikki.

"Yeah. I'm freezing," Jeri said. "I went to see Mr. Reeves's mom. I thought she might need someone to talk to."

"How's she doing?"

Jeri was dying to tell someone what she'd discovered. She'd much rather talk to Abby about it, but telling Nikki would be better than blurting it out to a reporter. Keeping her voice down, she explained what she'd learned about Mr. Reeves disappearing at night and withdrawing his money.

"Did you tell the police?" Nikki asked.

"No! It looks bad, but I know he didn't do it."

"If you don't report it, you're hiding evidence," Nikki said. "You want to get arrested?"

"It's not evidence if Mr. Reeves is innocent, which I'm sure he is."

"Let the police figure it out. That's their job. You have to tell them what you found out."

Jeri was sorry she'd confided in Nikki. She tried once more. "I don't want to make things worse for Mrs. Reeves. She's old and ... fragile. You never know. If I work real hard—snoop around and ask questions—maybe *I* can find out what happened. Then she won't have to go through anymore pain."

"Is that really why you won't tell the cops?"

Jeri frowned. "What other reason is there?"

"You want to crack the case by yourself. You think you're a junior investigative reporter." Nikki pushed her cowboy hat back off her forehead. "You're obstructing justice. By not telling, you put Rosa and everybody in danger longer. Why? This isn't about you, Jeri."

Before she could answer, Nikki jammed her Stetson down on her head and stomped off in the direction of the Two-Mile Stretch. Jeri felt as if she'd been slammed in the head with a two-by-four. *Stunned* didn't begin to describe it.

5

INVESTIGATING THE FACTS

Friday, 1:06 p.m. to 2:18 p.m.

Jeri felt dizzy. Did Nikki really believe she'd endanger people's lives for a chance to solve the crime herself? Did she honestly think Jeri was on an ego trip? She was shaking, and not just because of the cold. Needing some comfort food, she went inside the diner to blow a dollar on a brownie.

A pony-tailed waitress popped over with her order pad. "What can I get you on this freezing Friday?" she asked, pencil poised.

"A brownie, plus some information." Jeri leaned

closer. "The police said a man was watching out your window yesterday afternoon and says our school van never went by."

She pointed to a balding man in his midfifties, sitting with an elderly couple eating lunch. "That's Roger Atwood with his parents. He drank two pots of coffee while he waited for them to arrive last night."

The waitress got Jeri her ninety-five-cent brownie, which she wolfed down. She wished she had three more. Jeri patted her pocket, hoping the recorder was working right. Then she went to introduce herself. Mr. Atwood's eyes bulged like a bullfrog, his hair was parted down by his left ear and combed over the top of his balding skull in long greasy strands. He was more than willing to talk.

"Yes," he said, "I sat over there in the window from 3:30 to 5:15. I was afraid my folks wouldn't find my new house. I just moved out in the country. They were meeting me here to follow me home. If that school van had gone by, I would've seen it. Can't miss those ugly colors!"

"True," Jeri said. "You didn't leave the table the whole time?"

"Like I told the police, I never took my eyes off the road."

"I know this is personal, but ... well ... the waitress said you drank two pots of coffee. Didn't you ever go to the restroom?"

"No, siree." He paused, pulling on his fat lower lip. "Well … not for more than a minute."

A minute, Jeri thought, would be plenty of time for the van to drive by the diner. And yet, no one else on Main Street reported seeing the van either.

The man's elderly mother spoke up then. "Do you go to the school too?"

"Yes. My roommate is on that van."

"I'm so sorry, dear. What do *you* think happened?"

Jeri thought about everything she'd learned that day. "First I thought kidnapping. But today I heard that the van needed repairs, like its brakes. Now I'm thinking maybe the van broke down somewhere or went off the side of a cliff."

"Weren't the brakes fixed?" the older Mr. Atwood asked.

"No. Mr. Reeves reported it, but maybe it cost too much to fix."

Conversation in the diner died abruptly, and customers bent over their plates. A frigid draft of air blew on the back of Jeri's head, and she turned. Standing in the diner's entrance, glaring at her, was Headmistress Long.

Her back rigid, The Head marched past Jeri without speaking. Jeri groaned to herself and hurried out the front door and hopped on her bike. *Why* had The Head walked in at that precise moment? Wasn't she in enough trouble already?

From Dale's Diner, she headed into the Two-Mile Stretch. Legs pumping, she zipped past parked emergency vehicles, search parties taking a break, and knots of parents and teachers. Thankfully, the wind was at her back and pushed her along instead of stabbing her forehead with icy needles. She shuddered, though, thinking of Rosa and the others. Were they out of the freezing wind, or were they past the point of feeling any pain at all?

She pedaled even faster, rounding the curves that hugged the side of the mountain. At the other end of the Two-Mile Stretch, Jeri coasted into the Gas-U-Up filling station. Inside, she found the manager stocking shelves. Half his knuckles were covered with Band-Aids.

"Hi, Hal." Jeri glanced around the crowded mini-mart. Search-and-rescue workers were buying up the snacks as fast as shelves were restocked. "Wow! It's really busy."

"Sure is," he said, standing and stretching his back. "But I'd give it all up just to get those girls and Keith back."

"I know." She hesitated. "The police said you saw Mr. Reeves yesterday afternoon."

"Gassing up after their field trip," said Hal.

"Are you the only one who saw them?" Jeri asked.

"No, several folks did." He bent to lift a box of drinks. "They were parked here a spell while Keith monkeyed around under the hood."

"Why?"

"Engine trouble, I reckon. He must have fixed it, because they left then."

"Could he have turned around and driven to a repair shop?"

"No, I saw him drive into the Stretch."

That matched the teacher's story. "Thanks, Hal."

Jeri bought a package of peanut butter crackers and then headed back outdoors. The wind had picked up, and she pulled her coat collar up around her ears. She was unlocking her bike when Jake's TV van pulled into the station. Purple Hair got out to pump gas, and Jeri walked her bike over to her.

Despite being purple, the girl's hair was smooth, curled under, and neatly combed. However, the piercings on the girl's face looked painful. They weren't filled with jewelry—her lips, eyebrows, and nose held paper clips and safety pins. Chomping her gum, Purple Hair rubbed her chapped hands together and then stuck the nozzle into the van's gas tank.

"Anything new?" Jeri asked.

"Nothing. Sorry."

"I'm Jeri McKane."

"Lindy Pace."

"I bet you're exhausted after driving all night to get here."

"Nope. We were only in Rock River, not even two hours away." Lindy watched the gas meter, tucking her wad of gum in her cheek like a squirrel.

Jeri frowned. "You were in Rock River?" Hadn't Jake said they were in Connors and would have to drive all night to get to Landmark Hills by morning? Maybe she'd misunderstood him, but she didn't think so.

"See ya." Lindy replaced the nozzle and went inside to pay.

Jeri headed back into the barricaded Two-Mile Stretch. The wind in her face was numbing. Old snow had melted in the sun earlier, but was refreezing in the wind. She took her time around a curve. But before she knew it, her bike slid sideways and then slammed into the pavement. She and the bike skidded another ten feet. Jeri cried out as her ankle, pinned down by the bike, hit a chunk of rock or ice.

When she came to a stop, she fought back tears and thanked God that nothing seemed broken. She didn't see blood anywhere. Her bike rim was bent, though, and her ankle was already swelling tight inside her boot. She crawled to her feet and winced at the throbbing pain.

Hopping on one foot, she dragged her wobbly bike over to the side of the road. Now what?

Just then the TV van came into view. Lindy drove around the ice and stopped just beyond Jeri. She backed up slowly and opened the passenger-side window. "Looks like you hit a patch of black ice."

"I thought the road was just wet."

"Need a ride?"

"That'd be great." She struggled to her feet, her ankle throbbing.

Lindy hopped out and opened the passenger door. "Here, you get in. I'll put your bike in the back."

"Thanks." *And thank you, Lord, for having her stop.* Lindy would take her to Jake. Jeri was glad. She had a few questions for him. His story didn't match Lindy's—and Jeri suspected it was Jake who had lied.

6

ACCUSATIONS

Friday, 2:19 p.m. to 3:08 p.m.

When they arrived at the center of the Two-Mile
Stretch, Jeri spotted Jake talking to the police chief.
Maybe the ransom had been paid, and they were
rescuing the girls right now! She hopped out of the van
and gasped at the jolt of pain when she landed. She
spotted Abby and hobbled over to her as Lindy got the
camera rolling.

"Police Chief Reynolds," Jake said, "please update
us on the situation."

The officer cleared his throat. "From the beginning,
we set up roadblocks on major highways and smaller

back roads. Helicopters have flown over the area, using searchlights throughout the night. The weather conditions hampered the air search at times. Visibility improved, though, enough to see the lake from the air. So far, nothing indicates that the van is in the lake or surrounding area."

"Has that changed your plan of action?"

"We are presently reevaluating the evidence, yes. Even though no one on Main Street actually saw the van, I think it may, in fact, have made it through the Two-Mile Stretch and kept going. We plan to broaden our search."

"Isn't that a bit late?" Jake's voice was sharp. "Nearly twenty-four hours have passed since the students disappeared. Couldn't an abductor have escaped from the country by now?"

The police chief's eyes flashed. "I won't speculate on what might have happened." His clipped words were gritty, like broken glass. "We only deal with facts. When more become available, you'll hear about it." He pivoted abruptly and stomped off.

The camera swung toward Jake. "That was Police Chief Reynolds. Ground and air searches reveal that the van is apparently not in the area. Although he can't speculate, it is accepted fact that the driver, Keith Reeves, is the only one who could have voluntarily driven the van to some unknown location. There are four possibilities.

One, Mr. Reeves could be suffering from amnesia or stroke, though that's highly unlikely. *Two*, it could be a voluntary disappearance. People sometimes leave home to escape burdensome responsibilities."

Jeri gritted her teeth. She hoped that Mrs. Reeves wasn't watching this.

"*Three*, this could be a kidnapping, with ransom as the purpose. Although an earlier ransom note was a hoax, a genuine note could still come."

A hoax? What happened?

"And *four*—and this would be a true nightmare—we could have a multiple murderer who's dumped all the bodies in some obscure location."

Jeri thought she might faint. Why did he have to say that? The possibility had flitted around the fuzzy edges of her brain, but now he'd actually put it into words.

"This is Jake Philips, coming to you live from Landmark Hills, Virginia."

After Lindy shut off the camera, Jeri stormed up to Jake. "Why did you say that about Mr. Reeves? He's innocent! Hal at the gas station said Mr. Reeves was fixing the van's engine yesterday. It could be broken down somewhere. He *couldn't* have kidnapped those girls or murdered them! You don't know him."

"True." Jake patted her shoulder kindly and then clipped his cell phone to his ear. "Therefore, I'm not prejudiced."

She grabbed his sleeve. "You don't understand. Mrs. Reeves probably heard you hint that he's a murderer."

"You take things too personally. A reporter has to be objective."

"I know, but you're making it sound worse than it is." Abby stepped forward then and linked arms with Jeri.

Jake shrugged. "Ratings, my dear. People won't tune in to hear me say there's nothing new to report."

Jeri stared at the reporter. That was true, but weren't reporters just supposed to report *facts*? Things that had really happened? That reminded her ... "What was that about the ransom?"

Abby spoke up then. "It was on the news an hour ago. The note was fake. The police traced it to the boys' school." She squeezed her arm. "Actually, the police want to talk to you about it."

"*Me?*"

"A boy named Taylor wrote it, and he blamed you."

"I don't even know any Taylor!"

"Jonathan passed on your email alert to him. That email was traced back to you."

"I still don't get it." Jeri's shoulders sagged. "How did that Taylor get Heather's parents' email address to send a ransom note?"

"They said he found the address on Mr. Langley's business website."

"I can't believe it."

"Well, I can!" snapped a familiar voice.

Jeri whipped around to face the livid headmistress. Her words cut through the cold air like a knife. "You've done nothing but cause additional trouble—for the school, for the parents, for everyone involved! *You* invited that reporter, who is sensationalizing everything. The phony ransom note was written by someone who got *your* email alert. Do you have any idea how that ransom note raised the parents' hopes, only to have them dashed again? Because of it, Heather's father is now threatening to withdraw his financial support for our scholarship program. He provides three scholarships, including *yours ...*" She paused and then pointed to Abby. "And hers."

Each accusation was a bruising hammer blow. If only Jeri could disappear. She felt sick that she'd made things worse for people: Mrs. Reeves, the disappointed parents, and now Abby. She'd tried so hard to help! The pressure inside her chest wall felt like she might explode. What could she say? The Head was right. All her efforts to help had backfired.

Head Long stalked away. Jeri stared at the ground, fighting back tears.

Abby patted her back. "She didn't mean it. She's just worried. Heather's dad is on her case constantly. No wonder Heather wants to run away to Florida."

Jeri frowned. "Huh?"

"Yup. Florida. She has a friend there." Abby lowered her voice. "And something else. Mr. Reeves isn't the only one in that van who can drive. Heather can."

"No way!" Jeri declared.

"You know her roommate, Shauni? This morning she showed me a letter she found in Heather's desk. Heather wrote it to a friend in Florida. She talked about some partying they did there last summer and about learning to drive. She said she couldn't wait to live with her!"

"For real? But why leave school now?"

Abby's breath made tiny puffs of white. "Because Heather was copying Shauni's papers and tests. Shauni warned her to stop cheating, but she wouldn't. Shauni planned to report her on Monday, and Heather knew it."

Jeri felt a tiny fluttering of hope. "Has Shauni told the police? Or Heather's parents?"

"No. She said Mrs. Langley was worried enough already, and Heather's dad is a hothead. Shauni didn't want to mess with him."

Jeri hoped she never saw him again herself. "The police should be told though. Parents would rather think a runaway kid stole the van. I don't think she'd hurt anyone."

"Probably just dump them somewhere in the boonies … unless she crashed the van first."

Standing on tiptoe, Jeri spotted Police Chief Reynolds.

Grabbing Abby's arm, they pushed through the crowd to his side. She scanned the area, just in case, but Jake was climbing into his TV van. And The Head was clear down by the last parked car talking to two teachers. Should be safe.

"Need something?" the officer asked.

Jeri quickly told him what she'd learned about Heather. "I bet she's not dangerous at all. Don't you think the parents and Mrs. Reeves would feel better if they knew this?"

"Maybe, but I'd need to see that letter."

"Um, I don't have it."

"But you read it?"

"Well, not exactly. I—"

"Come back when you have some proof."

Jeri glanced at Abby, who stepped forward reluctantly. "Here it is." Her hand shook. "Heather's roommate was afraid to tell Heather's parents the truth about her."

"Because it's a forgery!" thundered Heather's father directly behind them.

Jeri jumped, and both girls whipped around.

His face was almost purple, and his eyes full of red veins. "Heather can't drive." He stuck his face just inches from Abby's. "What kind of frame-up is this?"

Abby's hand quivered, making the letter shake. Jeri stepped between them and pulled Abby behind her. Her own knees felt wobbly, but he couldn't hassle Abby like that.

"Let's move back, Mr. Langley," the police chief said.

"I know you're upset. We all are." He took the man's arm and forced him to step back. "I'll look into this. If it's not your daughter's handwriting, we'll know soon enough."

Heather's mom stepped forward from behind her husband. "It looks like Heather's handwriting," she said quietly. "And it's true. Heather can drive. She took my car keys at Christmas and went joyriding."

"No! You never told me this!" Heather's dad spluttered.

Not hard to figure out why! Jeri thought.

Heather's dad turned to the police chief and bellowed, "If you go after my daughter, I'll sue your police force and the school and your whole hick town!"

His yelling drew a crowd, including Lindy with her camera.

Heather's father pointed at Jeri. "I'll sue that girl's parents too! She slandered my daughter! I demand to have her expelled!"

"This mess isn't Jeri's fault," Abby's voice squeaked. "You can't single her out."

"Who are you?" he barked.

"Abby Wright." Her tiny voice dissipated like mist.

Heather's father gave her a mean, slanty-eyed grin. "The girl from England?"

Surprise written on her face, Abby nodded.

"I thought so," he said with satisfaction. "Fine. I won't single your friend out." His mustache twitched. "I provide

three scholarships for sixth-grade girls. You're one of them."
He leaned closer. "Correction. You *were* one of them."

"Lance, no!" his wife said, grabbing his arm. He shook
her off.

By now the commotion had drawn a large crowd.
The Head, whose nostrils were pinched so tight they
disappeared, took Jeri's arm and led her away from the
crowd. Then she turned. "That's the last straw. Stop talking
to the parents. Stop giving interviews. Stop 'helping.'" She
bent down and stared into Jeri's eyes. *"Leave the area now."*

Jeri was too shaken to reply. From out of nowhere, Ms.
Carter appeared and put an arm around her. "I'll find
other things for her to do," she assured the headmistress.
"Come along." They walked several yards away before she
whispered, "I'm sorry. Everyone's nerves are stretched so
tight. Miss Barbara can take you back to the dorm."

"Okay."

"Can you do me a favor when you get there?" asked
Ms. Carter.

Jeri nodded, staring at her boots. Her ankle was
throbbing worse, and her toes had gone numb.

"Tell Houston I cancelled our trail ride for this
afternoon. I tried the Equestrian Center, but he's not by the
phone. Look for him in one of the corrals."

"I will."

Ms. Carter pulled Jeri close. "You didn't cause this crisis,
and you can't control what other people say and do." She

leaned back and looked Jeri in the eye. "I know you. You have a good, caring heart."

A lump formed in Jeri's throat, and tears threatened to spill over. She blinked them back. "Can I get my bike? The wheel's bent."

"I'll help you. I'm sure it'll fit in Miss Barbara's trunk."

Five minutes later Jeri was huddled inside the assistant's car, the heater blowing blasts of cold air. She'd never felt so defeated and unwanted and misunderstood and disliked in her life.

7
A SNOWY EXCURSION

Friday, 3:09 p.m. to 7:18 p.m.

Miss Barbara removed Jeri's bent bike from her trunk, and Jeri limped into Hampton House. The assistant grabbed a granola bar before returning to the Stretch. When Jeri walked into her room, she noticed that her answering machine was blinking. She pressed the button. Her mom's voice filled the room, and Jeri nearly sobbed. If only she'd been here to get the call!

"Hi, Honey. Sorry I missed you. I expect you're still out searching. I'm praying constantly for you all." Jeri frowned. Her mom's voice sounded odd. "I was told today that my company reduced my territory. That's a pay cut, but I know the Lord will provide. Let's pray for a *full* scholarship for you for next year. I'm not sure I'll be able to pay even half the tuition. We'll talk later, Sweetie. Love you!"

Jeri sank to her bed. She couldn't believe it. The very day she alienates Mr. Langley—the man behind her scholarship—is the day her mom says Jeri needs even more financial help.

Rubbing her neck, she listened to the wind whistle through the pines outside. She couldn't sit there and do nothing! Time was running out fast to find Mr. Reeves and the girls alive. She could at least deliver Ms. Carter's message to Houston. She pulled on heavier wool socks, then her hiking boots. Her boot pressed hard against her swollen ankle. Grabbing her coat, striped scarf, and dry mittens, she limped down the stairs. Outside, she made her way north across the snowy campus toward the Equestrian Center.

As she came around a storage shed for lawn mowers and snowblowers, she spotted a familiar dark coat and blue-and-red striped stocking cap ahead. "Jake!"

Jake stopped and turned.

"Where are you going?" she asked.

"The infirmary."

Jeri caught up with him. "Why? Are you hurt?"

"No, but some rescue workers are. Frostbite. Exposure."

"Miss Barbara said the windchill's supposed to be minus twelve tonight."

Jake whistled. "Frostbite's deadly. If your skin freezes, your flesh turns black and falls off," he said with relish. "Sometimes fingers and toes have to be amputated."

Jeri shuddered. "No one's hurt that bad, are they?"

"Maybe not," Jake admitted. "But if they get that bad, I'll be the first to report it."

Or make it up? Jeri wondered, recalling The Head's anger at Jake sensationalizing the news. However, she clapped her mittens together and stomped her feet in case he was right. She preferred to keep all her fingers and toes. "Where's Lindy?"

"Down at the lake, filming background stuff mostly. I drove the TV van up here."

"Hey, Lindy said you were in Rock River and didn't drive all night from Connors to get here."

Jake raised one eyebrow. "I never said we did. We were just a couple hours away when you called."

Jeri's mouth fell open. She could swear … Jake stared down at her, as if daring her to argue. Instead, she pulled the voice-activated recorder from her pocket. She rewound it a few seconds, then hit "play."

"No one's hurt that bad, are they?"

"Maybe not. But if they get that bad, I'll be the first to report it."

There was silence, then clapping and stomping sounds.

"Hey, Lindy said you were in Rock River and didn't drive all night from Connors to get here."

"I never said we did. We were just a couple hours away when you called."

Jeri clicked off the recorder. "I borrowed this from the media lab for interviewing people. If you *did* tell me you drove six hours to get here, it's somewhere on this tape."

Jake stared at her, and Jeri tried to stare back without blinking. She honestly didn't think his earlier comment *was* on the recorder because he'd told her over the phone. Hopefully Jake wouldn't remember.

Jake's voice was cold. "It's illegal to tape someone without their knowledge. If you use it, you'll be arrested." He left without another word.

Jeri watched till he disappeared around the corner of the science building. Then, head down against the wind, she plodded over to the Equestrian Center. She hoped Houston was inside the warm barn and she wouldn't have to hunt for him outside.

She shoved the sliding door far enough to slip inside, then dragged it closed. *Ahhh ...* warm air. She sniffed the hay and horses and leather. It reminded Jeri of summers spent on her grandparents' Iowa farm.

"Houston?" Bright lights lit the indoor ring, several inches deep with sawdust, but he wasn't there. She started down one aisle. Rows of stalls held horses of all breeds, who were mostly yanking hay from mesh bags or slurping water from buckets. Around the corner, she passed the tack room, with its rows of saddles, bridles, and blankets. The giant clock on the wall, shaped like a horse head, read 3:30 already. "Houston?"

"Yeah?"

She found him mucking out a stall. "Ms. Carter said to tell you she cancelled the trail ride for today."

Houston tossed a forkful of dirty straw into a wheelbarrow and then leaned on his pitchfork. "C-c-can't say I'm surprised." His face was all sharp angles, with deep-set eyes in shadow under his heavy brows. "Not with everything g-g-going on."

Jeri nodded, almost numb from thinking about Rosa and praying for Rosa and worrying about Rosa. Could it really have only been twenty-four hours since the van disappeared?

"Did you know Rosa was one of the girls missing?"

"Yup, and I'm sorry." He tossed another load into the wheelbarrow. "She's a nice g-g-girl, not like those rich snobs."

Jeri shifted uncomfortably. She knew he meant girls like Nikki who made fun of how he looked and talked.

"How's Prancer?" Jeri asked.

Houston removed his hat, wiped his forehead, and replaced it. "Prancer picked up a rock yesterday. He's limping a bit today."

"Rats." Jeri always rode Prancer. He was an older horse,

and he didn't try to rub her off against a fence or break away on trail rides and gallop off. "Is it bad?"

"Nothing a little rest won't c-c-cure." He grinned. "Or a handful of oats from his favorite rider."

"Okay. I think I will." Jeri recalled when the center had inherited Prancer and a dozen other horses last fall. In fact, that's how she'd gotten to know Houston. "Remember when I went along to pick up the horses donated by that widow who moved away?"

"Yup." Houston grinned briefly. "Wish someone would g-g-give *me* free horses! I'd start my own stable." He wiped his calloused hands on his jeans. "Well, if the trail ride's c-c-cancelled, I'll put the trailer away and g-g-go help with the search again."

Jeri waved to Houston and then went to feed a handful of oats to Prancer. Stroking his nose, she glanced out the window to the woods up the hill behind the horse barn. It was part of the Landmark School campus. Year round they rode horses there.

If the van *had* made it through the Two-Mile Stretch, couldn't it be hidden up there in the woods? The towering, thick evergreens could easily keep the van from being seen from a helicopter. After the police called off the search and got rid of the barricades, a van hidden there could safely drive out.

She patted Prancer's neck one last time and then looked

for Star, a small Morgan mare … and Jeri second choice. At least Star was short and easy to mount. However, when Jeri entered the stall, Star shied away from her, kicking over her water bucket.

"Whoa there," Jeri said. "Steady, girl." She held out an apple from the supply Houston kept in the tack room. Then she reached for her bucket filled with brushes, combs, and hoof picks. In fifteen minutes, Star was saddled. They left the barn, walked up the hill, took the gravel road, and then turned onto the trail. Jeri leaned forward in the saddle when the trail rose steeply, wishing she was on a relaxing ride, not searching for missing people.

As Star walked through the shadowed woods, Jeri was struck by the eerie silence. Jeri searched both sides of the main trail for human or vehicle tracks. She spotted nothing larger than small animal prints and dainty deer tracks crisscrossing the trail. If only finding Rosa and the others would be as simple as following tracks.

Star skittered and danced a bit, then settled back down. Jeri searched the area, but saw nothing. Had Star smelled another animal? All her senses alert, Jeri combed the area, back and forth, side to side.

Star and Jeri took a smaller trail, which branched off the main trail, and moved farther into the woods. But she still found no sign of the van. With it being overcast, daylight was fading earlier, and Jeri knew she had to get back before it was too dark to see her way through the unfamiliar woods. The icy wind picked up, and although the trees cut the wind a lot, it whistled and whined through the branches. She pulled her scarf up higher.

The whining noise increased to a roar, and Star shook her head and pinned her ears back. The roar reached a crescendo, and Jeri realized it wasn't the wind. She glanced over her shoulder. A snowmobile, its rider wearing a ski mask, zigzagged down the hill, heading right toward her.

Star reared suddenly, landed hard on her front legs, and bucked. Jeri was thrown from the horse and landed facedown in the snow.

Coughing and gasping for air, Jeri rolled over and wiped snow from her eyes. The snowmobile roared on down the trail and disappeared over a hill.

"You jerk!" Jeri yelled. *Talk about rude!* Jeri fumed. *Not to mention dangerous!* She could have really been hurt. And he didn't even stop to check.

Snow was in her ears, down her shirt, and up her sleeves. Star was nowhere in sight. Thank heaven Houston had trained all the horses to go back to the Equestrian Center if they got loose. (He jokingly called them "homing horses.") But that meant she had to walk back, and her ankle was sore.

Groaning, Jeri crawled painfully to her feet. She'd had one too many spills—first the bike, now the horse. Following the trail, she shuffled awkwardly down the hill toward the school. Just before she reached the main trail, she spotted some larger tracks. What were they? Fox? Raccoon? At least the black bears in the state were hibernating now. Then she remembered that bobcat's yowl. She picked up her pace and tried to keep her weight off her sore ankle.

When she finally made it back to the horse barn, she found Star waiting outside, her reins dangling. Thankfully, she had no marks on her or injuries. Jeri led her inside, brushed her down, and put the saddle and bridle in the tack room.

Stomach growling, she headed toward the dining hall. She was nearly there when girls poured out the doors and down the steps. They were finished already! Jeri sighed. Oh well. She could make something in the dorm kitchen. She waited till she spotted Abby and Nikki and then fell into step beside them.

"Where were you?" Abby asked. "I checked your room before supper."

"Long story." Jeri rolled her eyes. "Any news on the search?"

"Forecast is bad," Nikki said. "They're predicting a huge temperature drop and tons of snow."

"Man, it's already freezing!" Jeri said. How would Rosa and the others survive now—*if* they were still alive?

Abby held the front door of the dorm open. "I talked

to that camera girl with the funky hair this afternoon," she said. "She said Jake might get promoted to TV anchorman for the ten o'clock news if this 'scoop' turns out to be big enough."

"No way!"

"I asked her how they got here so fast," Abby added, "and she called it a lucky fluke. They were told to cover a story in Rock River, but it turned out to be nothing."

"Hmmm," was all Jeri said.

Purple Hair seemed honest, but Jeri knew Jake had lied to her. Had he set up a phony story so they'd be in the area? Jake had certainly arrived *first* and gotten the 'scoop' on the story.

She gasped when the logical conclusion hit her. How would Jake have known ahead of time that there would be a sensational story to scoop at Landmark Hills unless he was behind the kidnapping himself? Or at least knew who was?

8

CONFUSING CLUES

Saturday, 7:41 a.m. to 8:38 a.m.

The mood in the dining hall Saturday morning
was somber. It had been over forty hours since the
van disappeared, and there was no break in the case.
Jeri poked at her blueberry pancakes. Even though
they were her favorite breakfast food, she could only
swallow a few bites.

They were nearly done when Headmistress Long
stood. "Attention, please. We have a hopeful develop-
ment this morning."

Oh, thank you, Lord!

"It appears that the missing girls are still in the

area." She paused and licked her lips. "A helicopter flying over the lake at dawn spotted two coats and a purple scarf by the water's edge."

"Rosa's scarf!" Jeri whispered to Abby.

"There was no sign of a vehicle," the headmistress said, "just footprints, according to the police."

Nikki raised her hand and stood. "What about the ice? Was it broken?"

The headmistress glanced at their house mother, who finally nodded. "Don't jump to conclusions, but yes, the ice was broken through. We don't yet know the cause."

Jeri glanced at Abby. They were thinking the same thing, judging by the horrified expression on her face. Temperatures had fallen all week, so the broken ice wasn't from melting. And if the hole was large enough to be seen by a helicopter, was it big enough for a van to fall through?

Questions bombarded Jeri's mind, pounding insistently. Did Mr. Reeves or Heather drive the van into the water? Did anyone escape? Why were coats left on the shore? They'd freeze without them! Or—*horrors*—did the girls no longer need coats? Had the kidnapper dumped their bodies in the lake during the night?

The Head cleared her throat. "Divers in wet suits are now searching the lake. We'll take hot drinks and food to the Two-Mile Stretch. The authorities hope that the students escaped and ran deeper into the woods to hide. They will search there."

Surely I'll get to go back down there today, Jeri thought. She just had to be there!

The headmistress moved to the exit, and Jeri hurried after her. "Please wait!"

Head Long turned, her face weary. "Yes?"

"Can I please go back today?" Jeri asked. "I promise not to talk to the reporter or any parents."

"No." Her shoulders drooped. "I can't afford any more unfortunate incidents. You stay away from the lake, the parents, and the press." The Head turned and walked out the door.

Jeri stood motionless as girls swirled past her, following The Head's instructions to go bundle up in heavy clothes. Someone laid a hand on her arm, and Jeri turned, expecting Abby. It was Nikki instead.

"The Head should let you go back with us," Nikki said. "You want me to ask her again? I could promise her that you'd stay with me."

Tears sprang to Jeri's eyes. Nikki was the last person she expected to try to help her. "Thanks, but I think it's a no-go."

Nikki studied her cowboy boots. "I *do* know how worried you are about Rosa."

Jeri nodded, then turned and headed to the dining-hall

restroom before she burst into tears. She was sitting against the wall, pondering The Head's words and behavior, when Ms. Carter walked in.

The house mother hesitated and then lowered herself to the floor beside her. "What's on your mind?"

After chewing on her lower lip a moment, Jeri finally blurted it out. "I've been thinking. I wonder if Ms. Long had something to do with the missing van."

"The headmistress?" The house mother blinked in surprise. "What in the world makes you say that?"

"She was mad that I called a reporter, even though it meant everyone in the state would be looking for the van much sooner. She didn't like me emailing people to look for it either." She rushed on. "I know this sounds dumb, but listen. If *she* wanted ransom money, she'd know which girls had the richest parents."

Ms. Carter rubbed the back of her neck. "That's all true ... but you've added two plus two and come up with ten." She hesitated. "Can you keep some things to yourself if I share them with you?"

Jeri nodded.

"This is extremely confidential, but I believe I can trust you to keep this between us. Ms. Long has her reasons for what she does. The school is suffering financially. Landmark can't afford bad publicity that might keep parents from enrolling their students. The headmistress is under a lot of pressure." She turned to face Jeri. "Parents and students demand more programs and better facilities, and it all costs money. That means increased tuition. The dorms need to be full to pay the cost of running the school."

"And if parents think their kids wouldn't be safe here ..." added Jeri.

"Exactly," said Ms. Carter.

Jeri laid her head on her knees. "I sometimes wonder why she works here. I mean ... she doesn't seem to like girls at all."

"You couldn't be more wrong. She *loves* you girls." Ms. Carter wrapped long arms around her legs. "Ten years ago, in a boating accident, she lost her husband and twin daughters."

Jeri caught her breath. How horrible! She'd always assumed The Head was an old maid. To think of her having a husband and daughters—to even think of her having fun on a boat—felt bizarre.

"After their deaths," Ms. Carter continued, "she threw herself into making good things happen for *other* people's girls. Landmark is her whole life now." She rubbed her chapped hands together. "I know this because she is my sister-in-law. Her husband who drowned was my brother."

"Oh! I'm really sorry. For you both."

"Later, she got me this job." She patted Jeri's knee.

"Just try to have compassion for her heavy responsibilities. She fears lawsuits from angry parents now. An expensive lawsuit could shut down the school. Of course, her worst fear is that the girls are hurt—or worse. The headmistress hired Keith Reeves. She holds herself personally responsible."

Jeri was speechless. She'd been so wrong about The Head. "I'll pray for her," she finally said. Had she misjudged Mr. Reeves too? And Jake? Did she have the good guys and bad guys all turned around?

"I'd better take the girls down to the search area." Ms. Carter got up and brushed her hands on her slacks. "Keep those prayers coming."

Jeri deliberately stayed in the restroom long enough for the cars carrying her friends to leave. It was killing her not to go along. She pictured a half-frozen, frostbitten, starving Rosa being carried out of the woods by a rescue worker. Rosa would try to stand, but her numb legs would collapse. She'd hunt for Jeri—who was her only family now that her parents were out of the country—but Jeri wouldn't be there.

Washing her hands, Jeri stared at her reflection in the mirror. The Head had always reminded her of the Wicked Witch of the West. Instead, it turned out that her two children died in some terrible accident. Jeri cringed as she remembered sarcastic cracks she'd made about her during the year. And all this time...

She finally headed back to the dorm, mentally trying to arrange different pieces of the puzzle to make sense. The school's financial trouble, Jake's lie about where he was when she called him, Mr. Reeves's bank withdrawal and mysterious evening disappearances, Heather's ability to drive ... Nothing fit.

Lord, who is the real enemy?

When she reached Hampton House, Jeri went straight upstairs and wrote an apology to the headmistress for any trouble she'd caused. She *had* taken action on her own, without checking with anyone. Even though she'd meant well, she'd created new problems.

As she trudged across campus to the main office, her eyes watered in the bitter stinging wind. A few flurries swirled through the air. Jeri fervently hoped the forecaster was wrong about the winter storm heading their way in a few hours.

In the office, the secretary was on the phone. "I'm sorry," Betty explained, her gray eyebrows arched. "I really don't know any more than what's on TV." A small portable TV tuned to a local news station sat on her desk.

Jeri stomped her snowy feet on the welcome mat and studied the secretary. Betty was fun—she painted on her own eyebrows, depending on the color of her outfit. They might be black, brown, plum, or gray—and thin, thick, straight, or arched. She changed them like she changed earrings.

Betty hung up and slumped in her swivel chair. "The phone hasn't stopped ringing since seven a.m." She got a bottle of aspirin from her purse and a cup of water from the cooler.

Jeri studied the fundraiser poster above the cooler. "So, which dorm is ahead in the competition?"

"No idea. I've been too busy since Thursday night to count the money that was turned in."

Jeri shifted from one foot to the other. "I have a note for Headmistress Long. It's personal."

"Oh. Well, just leave it in her office, in the middle of her desk." She pointed to a door near the visitors' chairs. "It'll get lost if you leave it on *my* desk."

"Okay." Jeri opened the door and stepped into the dim room. Gauzy maroon curtains filtered the light from outside. She tiptoed across thick carpet and dropped her note on the massive—and extremely tidy—polished desk.

Back in the reception room, Betty grabbed her purse and stood. "Jeri, could you do me a big, big favor? Answer the phone while I run to the restroom? I'm gonna bust. I need a snack too."

"Um, sure. If someone calls, what do I say?"

"Just say, 'Landmark School for Girls, Main Office.' Say that you're the answering service and take a message. I'll call people back."

"Okay." Jeri sat down behind the desk.

"You're a lifesaver, hon." And Betty trotted down the hall.

On the TV, Jeri watched the weatherman's special bulletin about the winter storm coming. If only the girls were rescued before it came! A few minutes later, a phone rang. Jeri reached for it and then realized it was coming from The Head's office. *Must be a private line.* It rang and rang. Betty had said to answer the phone. Did she mean both of them?

Jeri ran into the office and grabbed the receiver. Before she could give her greeting, a raspy male voice on the other end spoke. "I have some information. Talk to me, or I'll expose what's going on. You have my number." He hung up.

Jeri dropped the phone as if it had bitten her. *Who was that?* He must have assumed the headmistress had answered. "Expose what's going on" sounded like a threat—like blackmail! That voice was vaguely familiar. Could it have been Jake?

She hurried out of the private office and closed the door. She probably wasn't even supposed to be in there. She was back at Betty's desk when the secretary reappeared with a candy bar. "Thanks, hon. Did my phone ring?"

Her phone? "No. No, it didn't." Jeri felt her face go red. She hated lying to her.

Outside again, she barely felt the wind. Who had left that threatening message? It sure didn't sound like a ransom call, but what could it mean? Should she tell The Head … and upset her even more? She already had mountains of problems to solve without adding a blackmailer to the list.

9

A NUDGE IN THE RIGHT DIRECTION

Saturday, 8:39 a.m. to 10:23 a.m.

Back in her room, Jeri was desperate to *do* something, *anything*, to help find Rosa and the others. She wanted to defy the headmistress and head back to the lake. They might be close to finding the girls. Rosa just had to be alive.

Lord, can't I go back there? Isn't there something else I can do? She paced, still limping, while she prayed and waited for some kind of direction or idea. One of her mom's often-quoted verses came to her about how God "acts on behalf of those who wait for him." Why did waiting have to be so *hard* though?

But she waited. Eventually her heart stopped pounding, and her mind settled down. She was filled with an incredible sense that God was in charge of everything that was happening—that he had things under his control. Then a thought passed through her mind: *Go back to the woods.*

Holding her breath, Jeri waited. Was this a prompt from God? If only she could be sure that it wasn't just her own idea! At least she'd be doing something. She didn't get a chance to explore much yesterday.

Okay, she'd go.

She wrapped her ankle with an elastic bandage before jamming it into her boot. Down in the kitchen, she grabbed drink boxes of orange juice, a big box of raisins, and a bag of hard candy, just in case she found the van full of girls. They'd need some quick energy. She put it all in a heavy plastic bag with handles, which she planned to loop over the saddle horn.

When she left the dorm, the flurries were heavier, but not accumulating on the shoveled sidewalk yet. The sun was hidden by low-hanging gray clouds. As she passed the clock tower, it began to strike nine. She picked up her pace. Nobody was in the barn with the horses this morning, and Jeri was glad. She bet Houston was helping search again.

Jeri saddled up Star quickly, hung the food and drink over the saddle horn, and headed out. Soon she took the entrance to the main trail through the woods, listening closely for reckless snowmobilers. But today all was hushed, even serene, with lightly falling snow. She searched farther up the trail this time, but found nothing.

Leaning back in the saddle, she let Star rest. *Now what, Lord?* She hated this helpless feeling. Would she ever see Rosa again? Would Mrs. Reeves live with gossip and terrible sadness for the rest of her life?

Not if she had anything to say about it.

Scanning the area slowly, Jeri peered into the shadows cast by the brush and scrubby trees. The walnut and buckeye trees—she remembered them from science class—were too thin to hide the van. Massive evergreens much farther up the slope, however, swept low and touched the ground. A cluster of them could hide the van easily, but could anyone actually drive it up there? She didn't know how they could, but puzzling out the clues helped her focus on something besides how much Rosa must be suffering.

She thought about how Jake had gotten her interested in investigative reporting. She didn't like how Jake dramatized the news, but she *did* like putting odd bits of information together, discovering things, solving problems, and helping people.

Star pawed the ground while Jeri reflected on what to do next. Flurries thickened and turned to clumps of flakes. She found herself squinting through swirling snow kicked up by intermittent gusts of wind. She felt cut off, as if she were inside the unreal world of a snow globe. As she stared, the trees to her left moved, shifted. She blinked the flakes off her eyelashes and then looked again, her eyes finally seeing the shifting shapes.

Staring at her from the underbrush were three full-grown deer. They stood like statues; their backs looked as if they'd been dusted with powdered sugar. How perfectly they blended in for their own protection. Even now, their antlers seemed made of twigs and branches.

She hadn't seen them a moment ago. Yet they'd been there, right in front of her!

What else was right in front of her that she wasn't seeing? Was there something obvious about the missing van that she'd overlooked? The police assumed the van was in the lake or had been driven away by a kidnapper. Jeri herself wondered if Heather had knocked Mr. Reeves out and stolen the van.

But what if they were all overlooking something else right in front of them?

Like ... what if the van hadn't actually gone *anywhere*? What if—like the deer—it had blended into its surroundings?

She slipped from the saddle, wincing as she landed on her foot with the sore ankle. She petted Star's nose and pulled an apple from her pocket. Star crunched the whole thing in one bite, then nibbled up the pieces that fell to the snowy ground. Jeri was startled to realize that a new inch of snow had already accumulated. She ran a hand down Star's neck and chest, and her fingers felt the rippled scar. As a foal he'd been snagged by barbed-wire fence. She'd noticed it the day she went with Houston to pick up the horse.

Last fall they'd gone to a farm nearby to get a dozen horses for the school, donated by a woman whose husband had died. She had wanted to move to Arizona. When no one bought her farm or the horses, she decided to give away the animals and move anyway.

Jeri wondered. Was the farm still abandoned? It was just three miles down the paved road. An idea grabbed her, and she breathed rapidly. Was it possible that the van was hidden in an empty barn there? If so, that would explain why the roadblocks hadn't turned up anything. Maybe the kidnappers hadn't gone any farther than down the road from the school!

Jeri hurled herself back up into the saddle. She knew the chances of finding them at the farm were very slim, but she had to check it out. With the snow heavier and visibility shrinking by the minute, it was now or never.

She trotted down the remaining quarter mile of trail, turned right, and then headed down the main road at a gallop. One hand held the reins and the saddle horn; her other hand gripped Star's streaming mane. She knew it wasn't correct form—Nikki would hoot if she saw her—but Jeri held on for dear life. She flew down the road, woods passing by in a blur.

Star's horseshoes made a terrific racket, despite the fresh snow. If the kidnappers actually *were* at the abandoned farm, they'd hear her coming long before they spotted her. She thought the farm was down the next hill and just around the corner, then over a wooden bridge. Two more miles at the most. If Jeri recalled correctly, the farm was surrounded by trees that towered over the house, a huge barn, and several outbuildings.

After about a mile, she slowed and turned off the paved road so the snow would muffle the clattering hoofbeats. She headed straight into the woods until she could no longer see the main road, then angled left through the trees and started down the hill. She planned to circle around and come in behind the barn. If the kidnappers were holed up there, the road was undoubtedly guarded. No one should be watching the woods behind the barn though.

Picking her way through the trees and snow-covered underbrush, Jeri wondered what—if anything—the divers had found at the lake. She'd give her right arm for a cell phone right now. It was blizzarding, no one knew where she was, and there was no way to communicate. Unease nagged at her. Was she being guided by God ... or doing something stupid?

Progress was slower now, with the blowing snow obscuring her vision. Pressing on deeper into the woods, she fought down terror that threatened to engulf her.

Courage, her mom used to say, didn't mean you felt no fear. It meant doing something while afraid. As Jeri pushed on, determined to find the missing girls, she understood her mom's words like never before.

Star halted when they came to the edge of a ravine. Jeri hoped the wide gully below would lead her to the farm. Leaning back in the saddle, she rode Star down the slope. Turning left at the bottom of the ravine, the swirling snow hit right in her face, and she jerked her scarf up to her eyes.

Deciding to use Star as a shield from the blowing snow, Jeri slipped to the ground and walked beside her. As she guided the horse around a broken limb and a pile of brush, a sudden snarling *yooowl* rang out. Jeri swallowed a cry of terror that rose in her throat.

Star shied sideways, jerking the reins from Jeri's hand. She bolted up the slope and out of the ravine. Jeri scrambled up after her. "Star! Stop! Come back!" But Star zigzagged through the trees and was soon out of sight, taking the food and drinks with her.

Turning her back to the blowing snow, Jeri feared her trembling knees would buckle. She stared through the blowing snow at the trees around her, the branches overhead, and the thicket of brush in the ravine. Where had that yowl come from? Was there any chance it was only the howling wind?

No, it had to be that bobcat! Nikki said their dens

could be in hollow logs or brush piles or under rock ledges. Nikki had also said bobcats rested on low overhanging tree branches, and their mottled fur made great camouflage. With everything blanketed in white, though, it was impossible to distinguish anything. What if the house mother was wrong? What if bobcats *did* attack people? Nikki said they were meat eaters, that they stalked their victims and pounced on them!

Dear Lord, protect me!

Jeri looked to the left and right. No bobcat—at least that she could see. Snow clumped on her eyelashes, and she brushed it away, trying to get her bearings. The swirling snow messed with her sense of direction. She was still pretty sure the farm was to her left. Or was it? Fear trickled down her backbone like drops of icy water.

Star had gone back toward the road. Her hoofprints clearly marked the path, but only for a very short time. The heavy snow was already covering them. What should she do? Jeri knew her own best chance of survival would be to immediately follow Star's tracks back to the school. And yet, if Rosa and the others were trapped in that freezing barn, she couldn't abandon them.

She had to keep moving ahead. She had to try.

Back down in the ravine, she trudged on, head down, forcing herself to put one foot in front of the other. She fought against the thick brush and flattened weeds that pulled at her legs and scratched and jabbed her. Once she tripped on a hidden root and went face first in a drift.

With snow down her neck and in her eyes, she crawled to a nearby pile of logs and flopped down.

At that moment, a blurry form flashed out of the log pile, and Jeri jumped up. A scream tore from her throat. A two-foot-high spotted cat howled, its long white whiskers blowing in the wind. Its yawning mouth revealed two long fangs on the top and two on the bottom. The bobcat snarled and screamed again, and Jeri's arms flew up to cover her face.

When nothing attacked her, Jeri finally peered through her upraised arms. The bobcat was gone; she spotted its dark shape running off to her right. Jeri collapsed on the tree trunk. Sobs of relief and fear convulsed her throat, but not a sound came out. She began to tremble uncontrollably.

Move! Get moving! Jeri said to herself.

Jeri forced herself to her feet. The winter storm fury seemed worse, and the swirling whiteout confused her. The ravine curved around. Was she still heading toward the barn or in the opposite direction?

She fought down panic that whispered she would freeze to death, be buried by snow, and never found. No one knew where she was, and she might die without saving anyone. Yet, the urge to keep going grew stronger with each step.

She stumbled and fell so many times that she barely felt the impact before struggling to her feet again. Her boots were packed with snow that numbed her feet. Each boot felt as if it weighed a hundred pounds.

Her burning thighs let her know she was climbing

steadily uphill. At the top, while resting in the shelter of a tree trunk, she glimpsed a large, dark-red building below. The barn! Even if she were wrong about the van hidden there, she'd be able to find refuge and wait out the storm. Slowly, slowly, she picked her way down the hill to the rear of the barn.

Three small windows in the building were encrusted with snow. Jeri crouched under the middle one, straining to hear sounds from inside. Was it music? She cleared a small corner of the glass. An inch at a time, ever so slowly, Jeri raised herself up to peer inside the barn.

At first she couldn't make out a thing. Then the main doors at the front of the barn came into focus. They were open a few inches, and a tiny drift of snow had blown in. Gradually her eyes adjusted to the darkness. What she saw made her catch her breath—both with horror and with joy.

The van was there. It was parked, facing the large front door as if ready to drive out at a moment's notice. Was there movement inside the van? With its tinted windows, she couldn't tell.

At a center pole that reached up to the hayloft, a man sat with his back to the post. His arms, pulled behind him around the pole, were tied together at the wrists. Jeri watched as the man turned his face toward the van. The profile was clear—Keith Reeves was being held captive by a person or persons unknown.

Okay, Lord, Jeri prayed, *now what?*

10

THE RESCUE

Saturday, 10:24 a.m. to 12:15 p.m.

Mr. Reeves must be freezing, Jeri thought, *even if he's out of the wind.* And where were the girls? In the van? Had they been moved to the house? And where was the kidnapper?

Without warning, someone in a fur-lined parka passed by in front of the main barn door. The second time he appeared, he stuck his head outside. Jeri strained to see who it was, but his hood hid his face. Unless she was mistaken, that guard carried a gun.

Crouching down, Jeri shivered violently and rubbed her legs to keep the circulation going. To her right, she noticed a back door. It was split in half so the top could open for fresh air without letting the animals escape. Dutch doors, Nikki called them. Jeri could get into the barn there. First, though, she had to create a distraction to make the guard leave.

She sneaked around the side of the barn, which was mercifully out of the wind, and peered toward the house. The snow was so thick she couldn't make it out. Between the barn and the house was a storage shed. If she could manage to smash one of its small windows, the guard should run out to investigate, and that would allow her to get inside.

What could she find to throw? A white quilt of snow covered everything. Poking along the side of the barn with her boot, Jeri found a pile of broken bricks. Some were too heavy for her to throw far, and others were too light to break a window. Finally she found two that should do the job. At the corner of the barn, she pulled her arm back, took careful aim, and threw hard. Good grief! She missed the building altogether! The rock landed silently in a drift.

One more time.

Two seconds later, the crash of breaking glass brought the guard out of the barn, running toward the shed. Jeri raced back around behind the barn; she jerked open the Dutch door, slipped inside, and then pulled it shut. After the glaring white outside, she was blinded for a moment. Music blared from a country music station. Breathing hard, she crept toward the middle of the barn where Mr. Reeves was tied and dropped to her knees.

"Mr. Reeves!" she hissed. "It's me. Jeri McKane."

She pulled a rag down from where it cut across his mouth.

"Thank God!" His Adam's apple bobbed up and down as he gulped. "Are you alone?"

"Long story, but yes." Jeri yanked and tugged at the rope tying the teacher's hands together behind his back. Finally she loosened the knot enough for him to work his way out. From the condition of his raw wrists, Jeri figured he'd been trying for hours to get loose. With heavy bags under his eyes, the husky art teacher looked like a zombie. His cheeks were prickly as cactus from two days' growth of beard.

She glanced nervously toward the open door and spotted a large portable radio balanced on a bale of straw. Between the howling wind outside and the music inside, at least their voices were drowned out. Pigeons cooed in the rafters, and Jeri searched overhead for a good spot to hide in the loft. The "ladder" to the hayloft consisted of several short boards nailed to the barn wall. Long ropes hung loose from pulleys above. Could she use them somehow? Maybe she could jump from the loft and swing like Tarzan to knock the kidnapper down when he returned?

"Where are the girls?" Jeri asked.

"In the van, but it's locked. Looped chains through the door handles are padlocked."

Jeri pressed her face against the window of the van that was open an inch. "Rosa, are you okay?" she called as loud as she dared. In a moment Rosa stuck her fingers through the window. Jeri grabbed her fingers and squeezed. She could see Rosa's tears, and she held back her own.

The other girls whispered excitedly, but Jeri put a finger to her lips. They didn't dare get the attention of the man in the parka. Mr. Reeves struggled to his feet, and his knees almost buckled.

Jeri grabbed his arm. "Do you have a cell phone?"

"No, they took it."

"They who? And what happened? Quick! The window I broke won't keep him away for long."

Just then she heard the guard cussing and yelling. He sounded very close to the barn. "Quick! Sit down!" Jeri said.

Mr. Reeves dropped, and she looped the rope around his wrists and pulled the dirty bandana back across his mouth. His head drooped. She dashed behind a stack of bales in a darkened corner of the barn as the guard appeared in the doorway. If only there was a heavy shovel or a pitchfork! Head down against the wind, the guard's parka hood shielded his face—and kept him from seeing her.

Dropping to her knees, Jeri peered between the bales.

There were small rustlings behind her, and she held her breath. *Please, God, no rats or mice!* The guard walked near Mr. Reeves and stopped. He had a battered look, with his nose slightly flattened. Her teeth started to chatter, and she clamped her jaw shut. Satisfied that Mr. Reeves was still tied up, the guard flipped on a hanging lightbulb and left again. He slid the barn door completely closed behind him. Despite the dim bulb, the barn was very dark.

Jeri waited a minute and then hurried back to Mr. Reeves. He threw off his rope and stood.

Jeri shook all over, from both cold and fear. "He'll be back soon. We need a plan!"

Lord, help us. Please! Jeri closed her eyes and held her breath. What could they do? As she waited, Jeri recalled how Gideon in the Bible fought and won a battle, using directions as strange as those followed at the battle of Jericho. His army attacked the enemy in the dark, carrying blazing torches and trumpets. The combination of light and noise confused the enemy—and Gideon's army won the battle. Could they use blinding light combined with noise right here?

Jeri grabbed Mr. Reeves's arm. "I've got an idea. Listen." She sketched her plan. He smiled grimly and nodded agreement.

Through the open window, Mr. Reeves gave the girls in the van their instructions. "Everyone in place now," he said.

"Wait," Jeri said. "Tell me what happened. Quick!"

"We were nearly home from the field trip," Mr. Reeves said. "Halfway through the Stretch, a big trailer truck was stopped. A guy I'd never seen before was squatting by it. I figured the truck had broken down."

"Then what?"

"I stopped and offered the man a ride into town, and he pulled a gun! A second guy in a ski mask opened the back of the trailer truck and let down a ramp. The first guy—that guard in the parka—took my phone. Then he held a gun on us until I drove up the ramp into the back of the trailer truck."

"Oh no!"

"I considered making a break, but I was afraid he'd open fire on the students. So I drove in, and he got in the van with us, and then the truck was closed." He shivered. "The silent guy drove us here. And you'll never guess who he is."

"You *know* him?"

"You do too. The guy from the stables, Houston."

Jeri's mouth dropped open. "No way! He's been helping search for the van!"

"Clever of him," Mr. Reeves said. "But he comes here too, on a snowmobile. They take turns sleeping and guarding us."

Houston? Jeri couldn't believe it. Was *he* the snowmobiler who spooked her horse on the trail?

"Hurry. Get in place," Mr. Reeves said. He went to sit

by his pole, replaced his gag, and pretended to be tied up. Jeri turned off the overhead light, silenced the radio, and crouched behind the van in nearly total darkness. Peering around the rear fender, she stared at the barn door.

Waiting.

Listening to the pounding of her own heart.

All was quiet. Then suddenly the door screeched open just far enough for a man to slip through. He stomped his snowy feet and threw back his parka hood. From his stocking cap hung greasy gray hair, reminding Jeri of mop strings. A thin shaft of weak sunlight shone across the floor on Mr. Reeves, still sitting by the post.

The man glanced at the lightbulb, then the silent radio. "What the—"

Jeri slapped the van. On signal, the horn blasted and kept honking while the headlights flashed on and off repeatedly. The kidnapper whipped around toward the van.

Behind him, Mr. Reeves jumped up and lunged at the abductor's legs, toppling him over backwards. Jeri dashed forward, kicked the man's gun under the van, and then jumped on his stomach. Rolling from side to side, the man tried to throw her off, but by then Mr. Reeves was on him too.

The abductor jerked and cracked his head on the cement floor. Stunned and groaning, he barely moved as Mr. Reeves tied his hands and feet with the rope that had been used on him. Jeri gasped for breath, but then wrinkled her nose. Up close, the kidnapper smelled like he'd been hibernating all winter in a musty cave.

Still breathing hard, Jeri peered out into the storm. Had the honking attracted Houston's attention? She still couldn't believe he was a kidnapper! It took all her strength to pull the door shut. Mr. Reeves fished in the man's pockets and found the padlock key and cell phone. Then he crawled under the van to retrieve the gun. "Just in case," he said.

They ran to let the girls out. Four girls had their faces pressed to the inside of the window, but Jeri couldn't see Rosa. When she pulled the chain from the door handles and freed the doors, they were thrown open and girls tumbled out.

"Finally!" "Jeri, how did you find us?" "Are we safe?" "What happened?" "Where are the kidnappers? Did we get them?" "Is Mr. Reeves okay?" The babble of voices filled the air, but Jeri was only listening for one voice: Rosa's. Last one out of the van, Rosa fell into Jeri's arms so hard they both nearly toppled over. They hugged, but Jeri knew they might not have a lot of time.

"Quiet, everybody," Mr. Reeves said. "The danger isn't over yet. We don't know where Houston is."

Heather Langley pulled her leather jacket tighter around her. "I couldn't believe it was him when he took off the ski mask." She raked bitten nails through hair that looked like it had been attacked with hedge clippers.

"He was nice though," Rosa said, still clinging to Jeri. "He gave us lots of food and soda and blankets."

"I couldn't believe it was Houston either," Mr. Reeves said, "until I overheard them talking. Houston wants to open his own stable out west. They expected to collect a lot of money today before leaving the state. Ransom money, I guess."

"But they didn't send any ransom note." Jeri hugged her best friend close. "Things don't add up."

"Why? What happened?" Mr. Reeves asked.

"They planted phony evidence to make people think you all were in the lake." She glanced toward the tied-up man. "You were seen in the middle of the Stretch, but you didn't come out the other end. Rescue workers searched Thursday night and yesterday, but finally gave up at the lake. Then early this morning some coats and Rosa's scarf were found by the edge of the lake, so the teachers and search teams went back to hunt some more. Divers in wet suits even searched the lake."

"That's why Houston swiped my scarf?" Rosa frowned. "I don't get it. Why bother to do all that?"

Jeri frowned. "Maybe we're wrong about them wanting ransom money. What else could they gain by kidnapping you guys?"

Then it hit her. *Of course!*

Thanks to people wanting to help, the campus was

deserted. Teachers had joined the search parties, and students were either passing out hot food or confined for their own safety to the dorms. Betty, the secretary, was all alone with the fundraiser money still in the school safe. All the matching donations from parents and businesses would be there by now too. No wonder Houston had so many ideas to raise money for the new riding ring! What if the real purpose of kidnapping the girls was to get everyone away from the school? Then the money could be stolen with little trouble or danger—or witnesses.

"Mr. Reeves, I need your cell. Quick!"

He handed her the phone. Six silent girls clustered around Jeri. First she called the main office at the school. A series of squawks was followed by a telephone company recording: "The number you are trying to reach is out of order. Please try again later."

"That's what I was afraid of," she muttered.

Next she dialed 9–1–1. She explained to the dispatcher where the van was located, then gave details as to why she believed there was a theft in progress at the school's administration building. She was sure now that Houston was there, stealing the fundraiser money. He'd have to force the secretary to open the safe. What would he do to Betty if she refused?

The dispatcher thanked her and said several police officers would be at the farm as soon as possible. "They'll have to come on snowmobiles. The roads are drifted shut, and there's no sign of the blizzard letting up. We'll start the snowplows headed in your direction too."

Jeri hung up, turning when she heard moaning sounds behind her. Mr. Reeves planted a knee on the kidnapper's back and tightened his bonds. Then he opened the barn door a few inches, and snow blew in on gusts of wind. He started the van and let it run.

"Are we leaving now?" Rosa asked.

"I wish we could. I want to be here in case Houston gets here before the police." Mr. Reeves patted his pocket where the kidnapper's gun rested. "The van would be stuck before we got out of the driveway anyway."

Heather stomped her feet. "Can't we walk out? Jeri hiked in."

"I nearly didn't make it though, and the snow's even worse now. We'd get lost and freeze out there."

"Back in the van, girls," Mr. Reeves said. They groaned. "The heater's on, and you'll feel better."

The girls piled back inside. Jeri hadn't realized how frozen her fingers and feet were until she huddled in the warm van. She shivered violently, partly from cold and partly from fear for the secretary. Betty could be hurt—or worse. Even if she turned over the money, Houston might not leave her alive to identify him.

When three police officers arrived a few minutes later

on snowmobiles, Jeri and Mr. Reeves climbed out of the van to talk to them. Jeri was relieved to hear that the officers *had* interrupted a theft at the school—and just in time. The secretary said she'd tried to phone out when Houston demanded she open the safe, but the telephone wires had been cut. He'd taken her cell phone too. The secretary was all right—just shaken up.

Police Chief Reynolds brushed at his pants, encrusted with snow. "I should have seen that this was an inside job. Houston must have read the notices posted about field trip events and chose when to intercept the van. He was used to driving the huge horse trailer for the school. He just rented a truck the same size."

"I still don't get it," Jeri said. "He could have just quit his job and gone out west to start his own stable. He didn't need to do all this."

"I can explain that," Mr. Reeves said. "Time was running out for Houston. He'd been skimming the books."

The police chief flipped open a small notebook and began writing. "How do you know this?"

"I heard them talking about it. I pretended to be asleep."

Jeri frowned. "What's skimming the books?"

"He's been charging the school more than he paid for feed, hay, and tack. He even got free horses once and charged the school for them. He kept the extra money himself. He was skimming to buy his own place." Mr. Reeves stomped his feet several times. "Then he heard that the school was being audited next month. That's where someone goes over your accounts to make sure everything is legal. Houston knew the auditor would catch him." Mr. Reeves rubbed his chapped hands together. "That would mean more prison time. So he needed the rest of the money for his own stable fast. He'd planned all along to steal the fundraiser money. He just had to step up the timetable a little."

"Whoa! Back up a minute. *More* prison time?" Jeri asked.

"Yup. He did time a few years ago," Mr. Reeves explained. "He changed his name when he applied to the school. His accomplice over there is an old prison pal. Houston sounded downright frantic. He's claustrophobic from being in prison once before."

Jeri nodded, remembering when Nikki locked Houston in the tack room, and how he panicked before he got out.

After the police officer handcuffed the kidnapper and dragged him out to his snowmobile, Jeri turned to Mr. Reeves. "Your mom will sure be glad to see you!"

"I should give her a call now."

"Can I ask something first?" asked Jeri.

"Sure."

"Where do you disappear to at night that you won't tell her?"

Mr. Reeves flushed so red that he looked sunburned.

"Mom's worried about that, is she?"

"It didn't look good."

"Well, it'll be common knowledge soon anyway," he said, grinning suddenly. "My girlfriend in Rock River will soon be Mrs. Reeves. Last week, I bought her an engagement ring. I proposed, and Cynthia said yes."

"Oh! Congratulations!" *So that's where the money went.* "Rings cost a lot of money, right?"

"Yes, but Cynthia's worth it." He grinned even wider. "As soon as I knew she was the one, I set up a special savings account for it. I'll tell Mom tonight. She'll live with us, I hope. And now, if you'll excuse me, I want to call them both." He walked away while dialing.

11

FOR THE RECORD

Saturday, 2:30 p.m. to 9:56 p.m.

By two-thirty that afternoon, the blizzard had
died down. The heavy snow—someone said twelve
inches—had bent trees, loading down the branches
till they snapped and fell on electrical wires, bringing
those down as well. The girls were starving when they
returned to school, but lunch was delayed due to the
power outage.

Then, in an unprecedented move, Headmistress
Long opened up the dining hall in the midafternoon,
had a roaring fire built in its eight-foot-wide fireplace,
and invited the girls to gather there. The girls passed

around sticks and then hot dogs, and they crowded together to roast their hot dogs over the fire. The blaze roared,
providing both warmth and a cooking fire. Someone found
bags of jumbo marshmallows to roast over the fire and then
squish between graham crackers with a square of chocolate.

Mmmm, Jeri thought. There was no better way to cel-
ebrate than with s'mores.

Jeri stood shoulder-to-shoulder with Rosa, watching
her hot dog brown. Juices sizzled as they dripped into
the fireplace. Abby and Nikki peppered them both with
questions about the rescue.

"The police really brought you out on snowmobiles?"
Abby asked.

"Yup." Rosa giggled. "They wrapped us in blankets first
'cause the snow was so bad. When we got back, the drivers
were so crusted white that they looked like snowmen."

"Hey," Nikki said, grinning. "What do you call a frozen policeman?"

Jeri shrugged. "What?"

"A copsicle."

Abby, Rosa, and Jeri groaned. Rosa bumped Nikki with
her hip. "That was bad."

Jeri grinned, so glad to see everyone laughing and jok-
ing after the horrendous two days they'd all endured. The
dining hall was filled with relieved students, parents, and
teachers grouped around the rescued girls.

Glancing over her shoulder, Jeri barely recognized The Head. She nudged Rosa. "Get a load of that!"

"No way!" Rosa stared, open-mouthed. "She's wearing *jeans* and a *sweatshirt*!"

"And look at her hair!" Abby said.

Instead of piled high and starched, The Head's hair hung loose and actually looked messy.

"She's even eating with her fingers!" Rosa said. "The shock might kill me."

Abby laughed. "That's because everyone knows 'a Landmark girl only uses proper utensils,'" she said, quoting The Head.

Even more shocking than her casual appearance was how Head Long was acting. Jeri watched her move around the dining hall, talking to the teachers and the girls. She smiled. And she actually hugged someone.

When she saw The Head glance her way, Jeri whipped around to stare at the fire. Head Long might act differently with the others, but Jeri was well aware that she was probably still furious with Jeri—about calling the reporter, about antagonizing Heather's rich parents, and who knew what else?

A tap on her shoulder startled her. She turned to find the headmistress. "Can we talk a moment, Jeri?"

"Um, sure."

"Bring your hot dog with you. You've certainly earned it."

"Okay." Jeri got a bun, wrapped it around her hot dog, and pulled the hot dog off the stick. After adding a squirt of ketchup, she followed The Head to a deserted table.

"First," the headmistress said, "I want to apologize for my exchanges with you this weekend. Your motives for your actions were the same as mine—saving the girls and saving the school." She gazed around the room, her relief obvious. "I'm afraid I let the school's reputation and our financial status assume too much importance. You were right. We needed to leave no stone unturned to find the missing van."

"Thank you," Jeri said, stunned into forgetting her hot dog.

"And now I have an announcement to make." She stood and clapped her hands loudly. "Girls! Attention, please. I don't have a microphone, but I think you can hear me." She paused while the chatter died down. "The money that Houston systematically stole from the school—a very sizable chunk—has been recovered. He was also prevented from stealing the fundraiser money today. I'm grateful to Jeri McKane and Jake Philips, who were both instrumental in solving this crime and bringing it to its happy conclusion."

The girls whistled and applauded, and Jeri saw Jake and Lindy heading her way. She was flattered by the headmistress's words, but what did *Jake* have to do with solving the crime? He only reported what others told him—including her.

Jeri waited, not sure what to say. She hadn't gone after the kidnappers to get public praise or attention. And yet something really irritated her about Jake getting credit too. She watched him approach, feeling awkward. Her last two encounters with him had been very uncomfortable. He'd been rude to her—even threatening—and she didn't quite know what to think of him. But, she realized, she no longer wanted to be *like* him.

Jake gave her a quick hug. "I heard from the police chief what you did at the farm. You should have called me to interview you right at the scene. You're a celebrity."

"I only wanted to find Rosa and the others," Jeri said. "I don't care about being a celebrity." She paused. "Or ratings. Or being a TV news anchor."

He looked embarrassed, but only for a moment. "I think we would have made a great team though. Correction. We *did* make a great team."

Jeri bristled a bit. "Well, I told you things I found out, but I don't recall you telling me what *you* were up to."

He laughed. "Point taken. So let me do it now. What would you like to know?"

"When I called you late Thursday night, where were you, and how far did you drive to get here?"

"In Rock River, about two hours away. Yes, I lied about that."

"Why?"

"Because I was working on an investigation that involved your school, and I couldn't tell you."

"What investigation?"

"I'd been doing a feature on the costs of boarding schools in the state, to see which schools give you the most for your money. When studying the public records, I noticed that Landmark's equestrian program's costs were about twice as high as the other schools. We all know why now." He pulled a notebook from his pocket and showed her pages of numbers. "After Houston was caught today, I asked the headmistress for her records to double-check what I found. I warned her that I'd be going public with it soon."

Ah, the phone call she'd intercepted in The Head's office ... So that's why he was sneaking around on campus. He must have come from the Equestrian Center when she saw him. Even with all his facts and figures, though, Jeri didn't think he'd done all that much. Left to Jake alone, the kidnappers would have been long gone with the fundraiser money by now. He must have bragged a ton for The Head to think he'd contributed a lot.

They were interrupted by the noisy commotion of Heather and her parents arriving. Mr. Langley briefly searched the room, spotted Jeri, and headed in her direction, with Heather and her mother in tow. What a mother-daughter contrast, Jeri thought. Heather's hair looked like some rodent had chewed on it. Her mother, on the other hand, had blonde braids wound into a crown on top of her head. As they got close, she saw strands of silver threaded through it that looked like tinsel. Jeri longed to hide. She was in no mood for Mr. Langley to yell at her again.

"Miss McKane! I'm glad I found you!" His voice boomed across the room. Heather turned red and stared at the floor. "I want to thank you in some tangible way for helping to find Heather when your own police force failed."

Jeri blinked twice and had no reply.

He pulled an envelope from his coat pocket and then raised his voice even more. "I am, of course, keeping your scholarship money coming. No fear of that." He rolled back and forth on the balls of his feet. "*And ...* I am flying your mother down here for Parents' Weekend at the end of the month. These are her plane tickets. I will overnight them to her immediately."

Jeri couldn't believe it! "Thank you!" She knew Mr. Langley was just showing off in front of the whole school, but she didn't care. Her mom was going to come after all! "I'm really grateful for this. I know Mom will be too."

Heather's dad beamed again at everyone in the room, as if waiting for his photo to be snapped. Then he left, his family trailing behind him. Jeri watched them go and caught Rosa rolling her eyes. She agreed one hundred percent. No wonder Heather wanted to get away from him.

Later that night, after the emergency generators had warmed the dorms, the girls gathered in Jeri and Rosa's room to put together a special edition of their newspaper. It covered the kidnapping from Rosa's viewpoint. Jeri wrote about her investigation. Nikki covered what would happen now to the Equestrian Center. Abby interviewed the headmistress for a word of encouragement for the school.

It had been a terrifying two days. Jeri thanked God that everyone was safe.

When Rosa and Abby went downstairs to the kitchen to make them all some popcorn, Jeri began proofing the special edition.

"Hey, before the others come back," Nikki said, "I just wanted to say something."

Jeri turned to her. "Sure. What's up?"

Nikki scraped her boot back and forth on the carpet and turned her cowboy hat around and around by the brim. Finally she said, "I'm sorry for being a jerk yesterday." She stared at the floor. "I know after you risked your life today that you weren't trying to be a hot-shot reporter. You just wanted to find Rosa."

"Thanks. No hard feelings." Jeri thought a moment. "I think, though, that I *would* enjoy investigating and putting clues together. This was too personal though, with Rosa and the others in danger. I've never been so scared in my life."

"Maybe you *should* keep poking your nose into things," Nikki said. "You were awesome."

"She's right on," Rosa said, coming into the room with two tubs of popcorn.

"Totally," Abby agreed, carrying a tray with four glasses of soda. "What if we kept our little personal newspaper going by ourselves, even after the media project is over?"

Jeri grinned. "That's what I was hoping all along!" She turned to Rosa. "And you—"

"Don't say it!" Rosa held up her hand. "I have to get my part done on time from now on."

Laughing, Jeri threw her arm around Rosa's shoulders. "Don't worry. I've got your back. We're all in this together."

faiThGirLz!™
2 corinthians 4:18

BOARDING SCHOOL MYSTERIES

SECRETS FOR SALE

CHECK OUT this excerpt from book two in Boarding School Mysteries series

kidz

KRISTI HOLL

1

THE THREAT

Damp musty air hovered over the historic theater's orchestra pit. Notebook in hand, Jeri McKane carefully stepped around the six-foot pit, mounted the stage steps, and slipped behind the plush red curtain. Backstage in the cavernous gloom, she picked her way around props, stools, and other obstacles. Squinting, she read the antique movie posters in plastic cases hung on the putrid green walls: *Birth of a Nation ... Cleopatra ... The Bells of St. Mary's.*

She tripped over a coiled rope and narrowly escaped landing on a papier-mâché horse and pumpkin coach. She was at Monday night's rehearsal in order to write an article about the spring play, a Rodgers and Hammerstein version of *Cinderella.* Jeri's roommate Rosa Sanchez was the star. Although only a sixth grader, Rosa's voice at tryouts had been the strongest by far. Onstage or off, she had a bubbly flair for the dramatic, and she'd been a natural choice for the lead.

Glancing across the small stage to the opposite wing, Jeri spotted Rosa. She started to call to her best friend but then paused, struck by Rosa's odd expression. Bent forward, Rosa looked as though she'd been hit in the stomach. Rosa covered her mouth with a shaking hand as she read a note.

What in the world was wrong?

Rosa hurriedly stuffed the paper in her purse. Jeri started toward her, but Rosa straightened and moved to center stage, her lips pressed into a thin line.

Frowning, Jeri reluctantly focused on her original goal. Turning, she found the set designers stretching material across a wooden frame. Painted on it were streaks of moonlight and village houses with glowing windows.

"Cool painting." Jeri reached out to touch it, but—unbalanced—she leaned her weight on one corner.

"Don't!" shouted a husky girl with a red bandana covering her hair. "It's wet!"

"Sorry," Jeri said, fingertips covered in blue paint. "I can't see back here." She looked for something to wipe her hands on and then finally used her jeans. "That really is beautiful."

"It *was* before you pulled it loose from the flat." Bandana Girl yanked on the chain of an overhead light. It swung back and forth, causing shadows to jump and leap across the stage. She touched up the smear with the tail of her T-shirt and then stretched the material and re-tacked it to the corner.

"Hey, I'm writing an article for the paper," Jeri explained, trying to sound important. "What's that wooden thing called again?"

"A flat." The girl pointed to other scenery painted on screens suspended from the ceiling. "Those are called backdrops. You raise and lower them with pulleys." Her eyes glinted. *"Don't touch the pulleys."*

"No problem," Jeri said.

Jeri turned in a slow circle. Although it smelled musty, she loved the old theater at the Landmark School for Girls. The restored theater was on the National Register of Historic Places, and it felt like a museum.

Without warning, someone grabbed Jeri's arm and she jumped. It was Britney, a seventh grader, who had appeared out of nowhere. "Rosa said you're writing about the play for the paper. Wait till you hear my song with Hailey. It's *hilarious.* You'll *love* 'Stepsisters' Lament.' I play Esmerelda, and Hailey is Prunella." She tapped Jeri's notebook. "You want to write that down?"

"Um. Okay."

"Really, someone ought to write a whole musical starring Esmerelda. We need to hear the other side of the story! Don't you think so?" Britney shook her cascading blonde hair that reached to her elbows.

Jeri remembered from tryouts that Britney had auditioned for the lead. "It's hard to imagine you as an ugly stepsister."

"Stage makeup!" Britney squatted, dug into a backpack on the floor, and then handed Jeri two 4{dec63} x 6{dec63} glossy photos. "Keep these for your article. Isn't that some transformation?"

"No kidding." In the first photo Britney was her normal beautiful self. The second photo showed her in stage makeup.

Britney-as-Esmerelda had a wart on her nose, a protruding chin, whiskers poking from several moles, and a scraggly black wig.

Britney grabbed Jeri's pen and wrote in her notebook. "My name ends in *ey*. B-r-i-t-n-e-y B-r-o-w-n. Let's get the publicity right."

"Thanks," Jeri said, thinking, *Chill!* Apparently, Rosa hadn't mentioned that Jeri's article was only for their sixth-grade media project, not for the official school paper, the Landmark *Lightning Bolt*.

"Let's go!" the director said, clapping her hands. "Ready, Cinderella? We'll do 'In My Own Little Corner.'"

Turning, Jeri skirted the scenery and props and hurried down the steps to take a front-row-center seat. She glanced around the stage and finally spotted Miss Kimberly down in the orchestra pit. Only her head, thick neck, and beefy raised arms were visible. The obese twenty-something woman was an enthusiastic drama coach, but she looked more like a sumo wrestler.

Onstage, Cinderella was "locked up" in a tower room to perform her next song. Earlier, she and Salli Hall (who played Prince Charming) had both been totally convincing in their duet—despite their matching blue uniform jumpers. Jeri couldn't wait until her friends could perform in costume.

Jeri gave Rosa a thumbs-up, but her roommate didn't respond. Instead, Rosa stared into space. *What's up?* Jeri wondered.

A musical introduction blared over the loudspeakers, startling Rosa. She missed her cue by a couple of beats, and when she came in, her voice was weak. Jeri could barely hear her. In a thin, thready soprano, Rosa sang about her own little corner of the world and being whatever she wanted to be. Woodenly, she moved back and forth in front of the tower windows.

Jeri sat forward. *What's the deal?*

At the end of the song, Jeri clapped and whistled. Rosa stood with shoulders sagging. Miss Kimberly, dressed in black Spandex pants and a ruffled pink tent top, laboriously climbed the stairs from the orchestra pit to the stage. She closed her eyes for a moment, as if dizzy, and then lumbered over to the tower setting and spoke quietly to Rosa. Judging by the look on Rosa's embarrassed face, the comments weren't good.

"—and when you hit this part," Miss Kimberly said, raising her voice, "your body language and tone of voice need to match the words and meaning of the song. Here. Like this." She sat down on the child-size footstool, and it disappeared beneath her hulking frame. Although she sang the song without accompaniment and hit every note clear and true, she was breathless and pale at the end.

In the wings, Britney and Hailey snickered as the drama teacher sang about her own little chair. Jeri thought it was mean to laugh, but Miss Kimberly *did* need something more than a tiny chair.

Miss Kimberly finger combed her short, curly hair and announced, "Rosa needs to try on her ball gown, but the rest of you can leave now." She yawned and rubbed her eyes. "Good job, everyone."

Cast members gathered up books, jackets, and backpacks. Jeri ran up the steps to the stage area, waited for Miss Kimberly to go ahead, and followed with Rosa to the dressing room. "Are you sick? What's the matter?" she asked outside the door.

BOARDING SCHOOL MYSTERIES

A New Series from Faithgirlz!

The Boarding School Mysteries series challenges twelve-year-old Jeri McKane, a sixth grader at the private Landmark School for Girls, to trust God's Word and direction as this amateur sleuth searches for clues in the midst of danger.

Secrets For Sale

Softcover • ISBN 9780310714309

A blackmailer is victimizing Jeri McKane's best friend, so Jeri uses her investigative abilities to discover who and why. As the threats become more serious—to her friend as well as herself— Jeri dares to confront real danger face-to-face.

Smoke Screen

Softcover • ISBN 9780310714316

When an "accidental" fire at Landmark School turns out to be arson, Jeri Mckane is determined to discover who is setting fires—and why.

Pick Your Poison

Softcover • ISBN 9780310714323

When several girls get sick after a special dinner, everyone assumes the cause is accidental food poisoning. However, after further outbreaks Jeri McKane suspects the poisonings are more sinister.

ZONDER**kidz**
.com

Sophie Series

Meet Sophie LaCroix, a creative soul who's destined to become a great film director someday. But many times, her overactive imagination gets her in trouble!

Sophie's World
Book 1 • Softcover • ISBN 9780310707561

Sophie's Secret
Book 2 • Softcover • ISBN 9780310707578

Sophie and the Scoundrels
Book 3 • Softcover • ISBN 9780310707585

Sophie's Irish Showdown
Book 4 • Softcover • ISBN 9780310707592

Sophie's First Dance?
Book 5 • Softcover • ISBN 9780310707608

Sophie's Stormy Summer
Book 6 • Softcover • ISBN 9780310707615

Sophie Breaks the Code
Book 7 • Softcover • ISBN 9780310710226

Sophie Tracks a Thief
Book 8 • Softcover • ISBN 9780310710235

Sophie Flakes Out
Book 9 • Softcover • ISBN 9780310710240

Sophie Loves Jimmy
Book 10 • Softcover • ISBN 9780310710257

Sophie Loses the Lead
Book 11 • Softcover • ISBN 9780310710264

Sophie's Encore
Book 12 • Softcover • ISBN 9780310710271

ZONDERkidz
.com

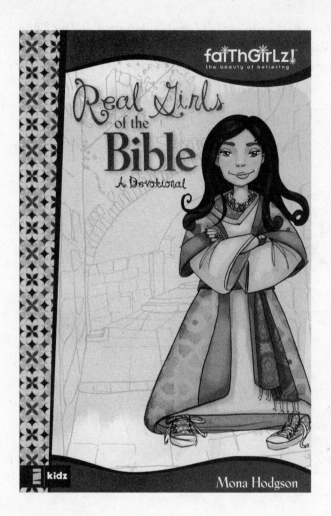

Real Girlz of the Bible A Devotional

Softcover • ISBN 9780310713388

This devotional includes stories of thirty authentic Bible women to illustrate the power of the girlfriend community to surround and support girls as they become real women of God, while emphasizing each girl's individuality and God's special plan for her.

Available now at your local bookstore! Visit www.faithgirlz.com

faiThGirLz!
the beauty of believing

Bibles

Every girl wants to know she's totally unique and special. This Bible says that with Faithgirlz! sparkle! Now girls can grow closer to God as they discover the journey of a lifetime, in their language, for their world.

The NIV Faithgirlz! Bible

Hardcover
ISBN 9780310715818

Softcover
ISBN 9780310715825

The NIV Faithgirlz! Bible

Italian Duo-Tone™
ISBN 9780310715832

The NIV Faithgirlz! Backpack Bible

Periwinkle Italian Duo-Tone™
ISBN 9780310710127

ZONDER**kidz**
.com

No Boys Allowed
Devotions for Girls

Softcover • ISBN 9780310707189

This short, ninety-day devotional for girls ages 10 and up is written in an upbeat, lively, funny, and tween-friendly way, incorporating the graphic, fast-moving feel of a teen magazine.

Girlz Rock
Devotions for You

Softcover • ISBN 9780310708995

In this ninety-day devotional, devotions like "Who Am I?" help pave the spiritual walk of life, and the "Girl Talk" feature poses questions that really bring each message home. No matter how bad things get, you can always count on God.

Chick Chat
More Devotions for Girls

Softcover • ISBN 9780310711438

This ninety-day devotional brings the Bible right into your world and offers lots to learn and think about.

Shine On, Girl!
Devotions to Keep You Sparkling

Softcover • ISBN 9780310711445

This ninety-day devotional will "totally" help teen girls connect with God, as well as learn his will for their lives.

ZONDERkidz.com

Faithgirlz! is based on 2 Corinthians 4:18—So we fix our eyes not on what is seen, but on what is unseen. For what is seen is temporary, but what is unseen is eternal (NIV) — and helps girls find the beauty of believing.

We want to hear from you. Please send your comments about this book to us in care of zreview@zondervan.com. Thank you.

ZONDERVAN.com/
AUTHORTRACKER
follow your favorite authors